Slipping

John Toomey

SLIPPING

DALKEY ARCHIVE PRESS

Library of Congress Cataloging-in-Publication Data
Names: Toomey, John, 1975- author
Title: Slipping / John Toomey ; English
Description: Victoria, TX : Dalkey Archive Press, 2017.
Identifiers: LCCN 2016049408 | ISBN 9781628971712 (pbk. : alk.
paper)
Subjects: Self-realization--Fiction. | Black humor.
Classification: LCC PR6120.O56 S55 2017 | DDC 843/.92--dc23
LC record available at https://lccn.loc.gov/2016031190

Partially funded by a grant by the Illinois Arts Council, a state agency

www.dalkeyarchive.com
Victoria, TX / McLean, IL / Dublin

Dalkey Archive Press publications are, in part, made possible through
the support the University of Houston-Victoria and its programs in
creative writing, publishing, and translation.

Printed on permanent/durable acid-free paper.

Contents

For
Oscar, Ruby and Luca;
All the love and the joy and the beauty

Part I

Novak and me

IT CAME VIA AN UNSOLICITED and unmarked parcel. Left under the cover of darkness. Hand-delivered to my doorstep but not to my person. Enclosed: a covering note; the audio recording; and a roughly constructed—though typed—transcript, telling of a man's life and of a crime. Not the kind of thing one ought to be greeted with of a morning.

Having played the disc, I ejected it. There was a shrillness to the voice. A quality that reverberated through the room long after it ceased to be audible. It hummed steadily, not dying in time as shock often will.

There was an unnerving lucidity to it. Something almost tangible. A voice with eyes; cold, apathetic eyes that held you in their unflinching gaze. Self-aware. Knowing how each word contracted or released around the heart of their audience. And it was obvious what it was purporting to be: a de facto confession.

The facts were broadly known to me, it having made the papers locally. One of the better rags had run with LOCAL MAN CHARGED WITH UXORICIDE. I'd have been reaching for the dictionary myself on that one had the tabloid sleazes, sitting on the newspaper stand, side by side, not relieved the story of any ambiguity, with their own headlines, puerile and predictably alliterative. It was all shock and lurid speculation and within a week they had the accused pegged - guilty and remorseless!

Case closed.

For my part, I had utterly dismissed it from the outset. Wrote it off as just another fast-moving sensation, something destined to fizzle brightly for a week or two before dying, inconspicuously and alone, in a factual paragraph buried deep in the middle pages.

Until it chose me. That morning, with that parcel. Brimming with all sorts of augurs and airy intrigue, nearly eight months after it had broken publically and apparently died, the inchoate story of Mr. and Mrs. Albert Jackson had life breathed into it.

I sat on it for a day or two before listening again. There were forty minutes of it. But it was incomplete. An excerpt. On the third day I listened to it twice more, back to back, with no interlude, and the more I listened the more attuned to the delusion of Albert Jackson I became. I acquired a feeling for the ebb and flow of his mind. Single sentences rang through the air in a hotchpotch of tones. In a split second, within one sentence, Albert Jackson sounded amiable, smug, arrogant, egotistical, tender, violent. His mind was like two straight lines of fast-moving motorway that diverge at the last moment, splintering in different though not opposite directions, only to converge again seconds later.

A desire to see where that voice would lead was what prompted me toward a tentative meeting with Professor Novak, the man who—according to the curt covering note—had placed this curio in my hands. On the basis of Novak's elaborate scrawl, I had him established in my mind before a hand had ever been shaken: an overly-serious and self-absorbed man. I imagined him so admirably committed to his life's work, and to his idea of himself, as to be unintentionally comic. And, of course, we can never entirely absolve ourselves of first impressions, astute or petty; it is the tiny prejudices and proclivities formed in as long as it takes to say hello that condemn us to tragedy. It is how a lover may jilt or otherwise humiliate us a thousand times over and yet redeem themselves in a glance, or the flutter of a fleshy lip across a cheek.

By just such insurmountable alchemy of the heart are bad first impressions cultivated, of course, which is what Novak and I fell victim to when finally we met in person. His pained and slightly undignified insistence upon referring to himself by the self-aggrandizing appellation, 'Head of Psychiatry at the Reil,' confirmed to me that a reverential lowering of my gaze would not have been entirely inappropriate. A thorny kind of relationship, one of unspoken animosities, but also necessity and shared cause, was engendered right there, as Novak met my scepticism with his own distinct brand of condescension and impatience. An unfortunate dynamic, it had the regrettable effect of immobilizing our minds and hearts to each other.

The Reil Institute, housed in an immaculately preserved colonial-style mansion, with a bright conservatory to the front and a patchwork of random extensions running off it in all directions, was built with an eye on capacity rather than aesthetics. Known simply as 'The Reil' to its patrons, inmates and perilously devoted staff – administrators, caterers, cleaners, nurses, specialists and sub-specialists – it was once a prestigious psychiatric facility.

Lying nine miles out of town, I knew it only by its faded reputation. 'The shuffle of passing feet, a few visitors speaking in low voices to receptionists, and the intermittent ringing of telephones, was all that interrupted the bright silence of the reception area. Although several men entered through securitised doors, converging off any number of corridors, and each made me look up to wonder, I knew Novak the moment I saw him. An impossibly tall looking man, thinly bearded with thick black and grey speckled hair, he was so obviously himself. Worn thin by the weight of his own sincerity, trundling across the patterned tiles, shiny and sticky-like on the rubber soles of his soft work shoes.

He shook my hand and took a seat, pinching the bridge of his nose and wincing as he sat down.

I organised my dictaphone, notepad and pen, and a few sparse notes on the table between us. Then, a minute or two having passed, he reclined on the cushioned material of the wicker chair, tapping his fingers on the upward slope of his thigh, while drawing the palm of his other hand across the unkempt stubble of his bearded jaw. There seemed in him a contemptuous reticence.

'So?' I asked. 'This is regarding the … local man … and his wife ? Yes ?'

'I'd rather not talk of it in clinical terms. If you don't mind,' Novak said, straight off.

I stuttered but managed nothing coherent, unsure what trespass I had committed.

'He's a patient of mine, certainly, but he's a man too,' he went on. 'You understand? He's coming back to himself once more. And that's going to be trouble enough. Realising. He's traumatised. I find it difficult... to be clinical. In the circumstances. I'll answer your questions, certainly, but you must hear what I have heard. Know what I know. He sobbed on my shoulder this morning. This man. Do you believe that?'

'Why did you contact me?' I asked.

'You're a writer, aren't you?'

'Barely.'

'And you're local.'

'I live locally, yes.'

Then, having thriftily explained the details of the case, he suddenly enquired as to what I thought Mr. Jackson's situation could possibly gain from my involvement.

'I have no idea, Professor,' I responded. 'My interest here is causerie. The whole thing was long gone from my mind until these recordings you sent me. The sort of thing I overheard people in town discussing. Over coffee. But it's not the sort of thing that interests me, to be honest.'

'And yet you are here.'

'Oh, I admit, there's a prurient allure to it. But I can take it or leave it.'

'Well then I advise you leave it,' he said, sitting forward.

I studied his grizzly demeanour carefully. 'Is there no doctor-patient confidentiality issue here?'

'It is at the request of the patient that his story is told,' he explained. 'So you *are* interested then?'

'Why not just ring a reporter? That's what I'm wondering. The local hacks would be all over this.'

'My patient is adamant that what is required is a fiction writer. He gave me your name.' Novak paused over this. 'How do you know each other?'

'We don't.'

'Well, Mr. Jackson knows you. Says he's seen you about town.'

'That's possible, I'm sure. But we've never met.'

'Never the less, he has asked for you. So whether or not you are willing to oblige him is the question.'

'He could do better. If it's a writer he's after.'

'No doubt,' Novak replied. 'But this suits me best as well. If it must, if he insists on its emergence into the public sphere, then it is better that it comes through some *artistic* medium,' he said with an emphasis that could only have been intended to offend. 'It is better that the facts remain questionable. Unreliable. That better protects me—all of us.'

'And he is of fit mind to sign off on this?' I continued, not pausing to weigh the dismissive inference of his words.

'Of course. You doubt me?' he scoffed.

'It's not a matter of doubt,' I told him. 'I need to know that the process won't be interfered with. If I'm to commit.'

'This is what he wants,' Novak stated plainly. 'You can be safe in that knowledge.'

'Fine. But why me? That's what I want to know.'

'Because he asked for you. I told you.' He thought for a moment, looking toward the door and out the glass panels and across to the wooded area at the end of a mudded track. 'There are two children as well. Grownup now. But kids are always kids. You should know that.'

'I'd be fairly confident no amount of words could smooth this one over, if that's what he's thinking. Fiction can't fix things like this, Professor. You know that, right?'

Novak said nothing.

'Why are you doing this?' I asked.

'That is immaterial,' he answered. 'Your involvement is the question we are concerned with. Whether you do it or don't, I don't mind,' he said. 'Frankly, I don't think you can do anything for Mr. Jackson. But he has asked and I'm obliging. Maybe it can be cathartic. Who knows?'

'Who will I be working for?' I asked. 'Him or you?'

'Him.'

'You don't approve though.'

He raised his eyebrows.

'What's in it for me?' I asked.

'A raised profile, possibly. I would have thought that would be recompense enough. For you. However, as I mentioned, we are in a position to offer a small commission as well.'

'How much?'

'I'd just take it if I was you. Say nothing. Count your lucky stars.'

'How much?'

'Four thousand. In two instalments. The first in advance, upon acceptance, the second upon completion.'

'Okay,' I said, leaning over and turning on the dictaphone. 'Let's get going. Give me what you've got.'

'No,' he interrupted. 'Turn it off. I will give you all that you need, but no recordings of me.' His colourless eyes bore through me. There was hostility and danger in him. Novak was a man who had seen too much. Who had watched men and women die, and murder and torture, and his punishment was now to live with the transfigured humanity of that knowledge.

'I need access to him?' I said, as if to prove I wasn't afraid of staring down the throat, into the soul, of the implicitly brutal. 'Access. Otherwise I'm out.'

'If necessary. When the time comes,' he conceded. He pinched the bridge of his nose, again, and sat back wincing.

'Is it a full confession then?' I asked.

'Confession?' Novak sneered. 'It's not so simple, Mr. Vaughan? Maybe you're not the right person for this after all.' He looked me over. 'But I'll tell you anyway. I'll let him tell you, shall I? Confess!' He shook his head disdainfully. 'You're a proper Miss-fucking-Marple, aren't you? How many books have you written, eh? One? Maybe two? None? Just some piece of shit manuscript sitting on a thousand desks, unread, gathering dust? Is that it? What gives you the right to call yourself a writer anyway?'

'It was you who called me a writer, Professor,' I reminded him. 'Now, are we to be talking or will I go home to my shitty manuscript?'

'You can hear what I heard, if you're prepared.'

I nodded my head.

Novak shifted in the chair and sat forward. 'Mr. Jackson provided, upon committal, by way of several statements and interviews, an account. Some oral, some written, they document the day preceding the offence and some of which we have already sent you. I doubt it would stand up in court, but I'm convinced that his account is faithful.'

I shrugged.

'Sit down with it somewhere,' Novak continued, indicating the table between us as an example. 'Put on the headphones. Listen back to it. The whole of it. Then read it,' he said, handing over several discs, the balance of the transcripts and the rest of the file.

'Your transcript isn't good enough. I'll have to do those again myself. All of them. If I'm to look at this properly. That's gonna cost you,' I pressed.

Novak dismissed the cost element, waved it away. 'Listen. Read. See what you see,' he said. 'Don't worry about the money. What we have, we have offered. Take it or leave it, as I said. And when you have done so, I'll answer your questions. If you have the stomach for them. Innocent fantasies—daydreams—that's how it began. It's not unusual, you know, for a man to imagine his wife is dead. It just took over. Listen. You'll hear.'

'Are there other statements besides his?'

'Some bits and pieces from the police records,' Novak said, opening a thin, brown file. 'You'll have to use it carefully, if you choose to. And what contact information I possess for people mentioned in his account. Use them if they will talk to you, by all means. But you may never mention me. Unless I am dead. In which case you can do as you like,' he said, smiling. 'You should know that Mr. Jackson succumbed to his condition. He is a victim too. Something took him over. One synaptic connection at a time. Something almost egotistical. A sinister delusion.'

'*Something?*'

'Yes. You will see. In heightened moments he is more … the alter ego—Albert The Lothario! The Troubled Genius, The Hero, The Put Upon Man, The Intellectual Powerhouse, The Wisened Recluse, The Brooding Love Interest, than his real self—Albert Jackson. It is a fugue, an essential disconnect inside his mind. Entirely necessary for the perpetration of the crime.

In these dissociative moments, when he is at his most bullish, he becomes purely *Albert*. You can hear *him* weaving in and out of the account. If you listen closely.'

As I drove home, the discs and the file lain on the passenger seat, I considered what all this might become in my hands. It certainly wouldn't be anything remotely similar to its original self. To anything Albert Jackson imagined it could be. Did he appreciate that? I wondered. Because I knew that once this began it could only become that other thing—a manuscript. A narrative. A story.

Something neither true nor untrue.

The narrative of Albert Jackson

One

... IT WASN'T THAT I DIDN'T love her. I tell you that for sure. With full certainty. There was too much love, perhaps, or love too pure. But it was not a matter of love's absence.

So where to begin then? That morning, I suppose. Although there is much more to it, you understand. Asking where a story begins is like asking where time began. There's always further back again. But since it must begin, let it be like so ...

I lay awake beside her, just before the inching break of dawn. Facing her sleepy contours. Listening to her breathe. A beautiful voiceless sound; her lungs heaving gently inward, her dark humps swelling and dipping. Like something oceanic ...

Yes, that will do nicely, won't it ...

Come the morning, in fussy daylight, milk splashed over the cereal and her spoon clinked on the bowl, chipping excruciatingly at the silence. I sipped tea, careful not to slurp, and read; my finger held at two inches from the tip of my nose, moving cursorily from left to right, across the grey expanse of the morning paper. Concentration straining to win out over interruption.

Her voice was not typically musical but was capable, none the less, of lulling me to contentment. Through familiarity and distant intimacy.

'More tea? Any toast? A croissant? My love ... Darling ... Sweetheart,' and so on and so forth.

But not this morning.

A shake of the head. And another. If only she could leave it there. But she persisted, as she always did. Persistence defined her.

A smile and a shake of my head.

Still more persistence that soon became insistence.

Finally, I was compelled to speak. And so I did, to castrate that compulsion of hers to provide.

'No, honestly, I'm fine,' I said.

I hoped this was us done and I could return to my sound-proofed mind. But she had more words to share with me, more words to which I hardly listened.

'Four o'clock, darling.'

'What's that?' I asked, trying to collect and disregard in one.

Damn it! I exclaimed. Inwardly, and perhaps a little outwardly. The day had begun without my consent.

'Four o'clock. My appointment. Should be home by five-thirty. At the latest,' she said.

Dressed, I turned my shoulder to the audience of the mirror. *Nice*, I thought. Lean legs, the shoeshined glint of my black shoes.

I patted my stomach, taut and spare, and permitted my reflection a satisfied smile. Tidy enough. Well-preserved. And that's none too shabby at forty-nine. I have not fallen to sloven-liness, as most men do. At ten and a half stone and half an inch below six foot, there are worse than me. Evading repulsiveness is in itself a success, at a certain age.

I shuffled the loose sheets of notes I'd prepared into a neatly symmetrical block and slid them between a history and an English textbook; held secure and protected from fraying and rumpling. With two exterior buckles I then secured the bag and left the house. One stride became two, then three, and so on, until my feet had grown full and purposeful.

For twenty-five years I have followed the same route, each morning of each weekday of term-time. There were periods when I drove, and another when I cycled, and then—recently—I began walking. But the route that I walk, daily, is the same route travelled all my working life; winding in and around the estate, a mile down the coast road into town, through it and beyond, to the school complex at the far side.

I had been walking months before Val wondered what had come over me. What strange impulse was this, she asked, to begin walking to work at the age of forty-nine? It wasn't what a man of my vintage ought to be doing. 'Or if you're to insist

on it, you should invest in a smart overcoat and briefcase,' she
said. 'That god-awful leather satchel of yours is spilling over with
books and papers, Al. Have you no pride?'

The weight of the satchel causes me to heave and creak, 'Like
some lamed farmhand from an awful Steinbeck novel,' Val enjoys
saying. And I like the literary reference. It is her tiny acknowl-
edgment of who I am. Of my passions, and talents, and taste.
That I'm not too pushed on Steinbeck either hardly matters.

What worsens the folly of my walking is that on a couple of
evenings I have arrived home soaked through, with dense glob-
ules of rain gathered and congealed at the cuffs of my woollen
suit; dangling and plummeting to the doormat, as I step inside
the porch, beaming like the child who has spent the afternoon
jumping in mud.

'Sweet mother of our lord, Albert, whatever has you walking to work again? Take the car, would you? Or buy a bloody
umbrella,' she said on one of those evenings.

'An umbrella, yes,' I responded.

'Why the walking anyway, Al? Having an affair or something? Should I be checking your drawers for new underwear?
Some young belle on staff, maybe, fawning over your aloof
angularity?'

She was irritable that evening.

'An affair, Val? Now that would be something,' I said,
engaged, back in regular time again. *An affair. An affair?*

We both laughed...

The walking began because I could not think. From the moment
I got out of bed there were voices and demands rapping on the
Lucite coating of my secluded mind; damp thuds and scratchings
of other people in my ear. I had believed that when the second
of our children, for whom I have an incurable soft spot, it is
true, had departed for college that a utopian tranquillity would
automatically descend upon us. Upon our house. Our life. I
believed that the noise would end when the children did. When
they ceased to be children, when they went off about their own
lives and left us to rediscover ours.

What actually happened was that Val's need to fill the silences became more pronounced, and inane. And when she failed to illicit conversation from me, the volume on her morning radio jumped a decibel or four. And not even adult radio but trivial breakfast shows with skits and prizes and too much music and too many sponsors, and all the gravitas of obnoxious adolescence.

It was for silence and fresh air, which is good for the mind, that I began walking to work.

By the time I set foot in the staffroom that first morning of walking, I was so rejuvenated by the experience that I resolved to sell my car immediately. So immediately, in fact, that I offered it to the first person I met.

Aimée Quinn. Our French-Irish English teacher, recently made permanent. She is a delicate (which would be the French in her, I suppose) and decent flower, with a long career ahead of her; only interrupted for maternity leave, a few years in the future, no doubt, after she marries some ego-laden fellow teacher, plucked from among our colleagues on staff here, most likely, or from another school in the area. I've seen this sort of thing so often before. It's inevitable. But she'll return to teaching out of a desire to be remembered fondly. They all do.

'Any interest in buying my car, Aimée?' I asked her, straight out.

'Sorry, Al?' she said, taken aback. 'What's that you said?'

She'd hardly noticed me in the small kitchen, a Teflon sweat glistening upon my forehead and neck, as she finished the last pages of some Ibsen play, head down, while waiting on coffee and polishing off a banana.

'Any interest in buying my car? I'm selling it. Knock-down price of... very little. It's a fine car. Good in all weather. Two years old. I don't want it. I don't need it. I'm walking from now on. Walking everywhere,' I declared, buoyantly.

'I'm good for a car, thanks,' she said. 'How come you're walking everywhere then?'

'Well, I walked in this morning. First time since... since a long time. It was refreshing. Peaceful. Invigorating.'

'Peaceful and invigorating? Seems almost paradoxical, Al.'

'It does, doesn't it? So you're sure you don't want it?'

'Yeah, Al. Thanks,' she said, smiling up at me as she took her breakfast through to the inner staffroom. 'But listen, I'll put the word out for you.'

Her face, caressed on both sides by silken blonde drapes of hair, and lit up from within by that slightly skewed smile, projected itself, uninterrupted, above the slow bustle of the room. I watched her walk away, shimmering in a way only the truly sentient can appreciate. She hung there like a projected simulacrum of perfection, for what seemed a longer duration than was plausible...

On the morning in question, however—many months after the first walking—I set a brisk pace. Within minutes I was out of our quiet estate and well on my way along that footpath that winds for almost a mile into the town's centre.

It was a typical autumn morning, the low sun sifting through September's plush foliage and blinding me slightly to the passing cars and people. The strange opaqueness of it, and the wet-slap-and-click of my dress shoes, rhythmical and hypnotic on the pavement, facilitated a retreat into my own thoughts once again.

And so I picked up the thread of my most dominant fantasy; me graveside, under an interminable misty drizzle, alone, watching over Val's weathered headstone. It bestirred in me a peculiar happiness, I might as well admit. There was potency to the free-wheeling sorrow. Beatification! The tears I imagined shedding dampened my cheek; I actually placed the tips of my fingers on my face, to feel them. And they excited me.

The solitariness of the scene invoked other images too, images that were less painful but just as pleasing; a breakfast in the family home with nothing but the rustle of a turning newspaper and the cocoa warmth of coffee in my throat; the sympathetic visit of the children, assuaging any threat of genuine loneliness, but never staying too long; the tender concern of an unidentified, and younger, female acquaintance, itching to be something illicit even as she consoled me on the loss of my wife...

These are scenes that have been teased and worked, you see. Over and over in my mind, over the course of years, though I can't be certain when precisely it was that they first visited me. But they come on particularly strong when I walk, or run or am at work. Lateral fantasies, you could call them, asserting themselves as the conscious mind looks the other way...

Anyway, to my right lay the sea, murmuring in the near distance, its ancient scent adrift inland. My heavy satchel strained in my shoulder and through to my ribs and down my thigh. Before long I reached town and was glad of the opportunity to stop at the local coffee house, despite realising that it would compel me to engage with the world...

However necessary on a practical level, the act of small talk is one that I have come to experience as increasingly laborious. Ours is a small town, as you know, and a teacher with twenty-five years' service under his belt finds recognition unavoidable. So the demands on me are more than they are for others. The law, the medics and the educators; I am one of these societal pillars. I have spent all my working life in this town. People will always expect of me, at the very least, a genial, *Hello..*

'Morning, Al, how's Val?' asked Terri, as predictable as you like.

'All good. How're your boys?' I responded. 'And that girl too, of course?' I then added, in a manner so pointlessly jocular as to be fraudulent...

Terri Carlson is somebody we have known since she arrived in town, a few short years after us. She cornered the market with the town's first coffeehouse. Other coffee shops, other businesses, have come and gone, but Terri's is a fixture. One of her boys is about the same age as our Jake, and she had three others, followed by a late-arriving daughter, all of whom have passed through my classes at one stage or another. None of them too bright but all fairly amiable...

'As good as can be, Al. The usual?'

'That would be great, Terri. Thanks.'

I fumbled with some notes and coins, playing at preoccupation as best I could, and allowed Terri to move along to the customers waiting behind me...

People disgust me. To be honest. I long to be alone, away

from them and their social pleasantries. Away from etiquette, as if anybody even knows what that means these days. Small talk, as I said, has always been a source of irritation to me but in recent times I've come to utterly detest it. To the extent that I almost fear it. Fear I might throttle somebody, or drop into a whimpering ball right there on the street, in abject exasperation at life's triviality. I have contrived any number of ways to avoid meeting certain people on the street. I plan departures in advance of arrival. I anticipate and prepare for my exits—appointments, work, emergencies, illnesses. You name it, I've used it.

In fact, even at home I have long been inventing jobs for myself. Just to get away, for a while, from the incessant aural deluge that is life with Val. I set myself fitness goals that necessitate my leaving the house altogether, for hours at a time. I have the dog damn near walked off its legs.

Sometimes I imagine an existence without such irritation, where I could observe and yet not be present. What I want is to be inconspicuous, really. Rather than invisible or alone. It's not that I'm opposed to society, or people, or that I've no appreciation of the necessary symbiosis between individual and community, it's just that I'd prefer to be there but not in the midst of it. I don't desire interaction with it...

Standing there in Terri Carlson's, avoiding niceties, I felt this wasn't much to ask. Without Val, for instance, who would know me well enough to say any more than 'Good morning,' 'Hello' or 'Pleasant evening, Mr. Jackson'? If circumstances were different it is conceivable that I could have sat down in Terri's coffeehouse, quietly observing the world, without ever being noticed...

When I could see my coffee at the ready, I paid and tipped...

I'm a generous tipper, as it happens, but I am not flippant about it. I'll pay for manners and courtesy. Pay a premium...

I had my hand out for the coffee before the lid was on the cup. Another premeditated exit. 'Running dead late now. See you later,' I said.

'Bye, Al,' she said, looking away as quick as she'd acknowledged my farewell. 'Next? Mary, how're you doing? How's your mother?' I heard her enquire...

More banality. The murderous, crimson flow of banality. Bloody, bloody banality! This is what I can no longer allow to just passively happen to me. The years are short, the opportunities fewer...

Turning right onto the Old School Road, there came a slow dawning of two realities, in perfect juxtaposition; the grey stump of the school buildings to my right, immovable and grim on the landscape, and the metallic-red glimmer of Aimeé Quinn's car, gliding by me on the left.

She curled into a tight parking spot in front of the dour boxiness of the school. I watched her lift and swivel herself from the front seat, reach back for a handbag and a sheaf of papers, and walk tantalisingly away. She had seen me as she closed the door and offered a cursory smile, that even from a distance of fifty yards, and through wrought iron railings, promised effervescent possibility. With what seemed like a glissading movement across space and time, I was drawn after her; eased gently along the path and through the gate and onwards to the front steps.

The delicate yet gargantuan scope of events to come had only begun to mutate within my deepest subconscious when I was interrupted by an objectionable voice crossing the car park in my direction.

'Sir? Sir, Sir, Sir, Sir?'

'Yes?' I responded, impatiently, turning but still walking.

'Can I ask you something?'

'Evidently,' I replied.

The boy's lanky emaciation, his hormonal face pocks, repulsed me...

I am victim to squeamishness. This is true. It borders on manic intolerance, to be honest. Ugliness sits poorly with me, just like that fellow in the Ibsen play Aimeé Quinn has been teaching. In fact, a certain commonality with Torvald Helmer had struck me for the first time several weeks before. We were in our bedroom and I was on the bed, incomprehensively glued to a ridge of wrinkled fat that quivered on Val's upper thigh as she dried herself off, one foot on the bed, and the towel furiously fluffing the underside of her leg. Torvald's great difficulty, of course, is in facing life's uglinesses. It is his core weakness and in acknowledging the similarity, I know, I am identifying a weakness in myself. But I'm only barely apologetic of it. Somewhere in my heart I suspect that it behoves us to expect more, on an aesthetic level. Polite acceptance of ugliness, slovenly appearance, is one of those contemporary diseases that society has surrendered too easily to ...

But the boy. Yes, the boy! Of course ...

He began to make his excuses. 'Is that assignment for today, 'cause if it is, I haven't got it,' he said, preempting my answer in the formulation of his question.

His cause was done no favours by adding tardy time-keeping and ill-discipline to aesthetic impurity, so I answered him bluntly. 'Yesterday.'

'What, Sir?'

'Yesterday.'

'Yesterday what?'

I stalled, one foot on the lowest step, one shoulder turned to the boy. 'It was due yesterday. You've already been graced with an extension.'

'So what do I do then?'

'You fail,' I said. *You gangly fuckwit.*

'Ah, come on, Sir. I'll have it for you.'

'When? When do you think would be satisfactory?'

'End of the week?'

'Fine,' I said, nodding my head and rolling my wrists and flinging open my palms, as if to say, *Is that it? Are we done now?*

'And I won't be failed?'

'Not for your lateness, no.'

'Nice one, Sir. Catch you later.'

Oh, fuck-off! I said. *Clown!* His unearned familiarity offensive in the extreme.

I ascended the chalky steps and made my way towards another mug of coffee. Within seconds the encounter was behind me and I was secure again, sheltered behind the breathing membrane walls of my intimate mind ...

Three lessons, roughly eighty adolescents, two subjects and

several coffees dotted the workaday landscape of the morning and yet hardly made an impression, so immersed was I in my own thoughts. It was only the boorishness of Nicholas Jones's gait, a shape and movement that never failed to stoke the passions of dormant revulsion in me, that disturbed the rhythms of the morning.

Students were filing down the corridor erratically—starting, swerving, shouldering, greeting, changing direction, leaving half conversations flittering in the dank air. But standing bold and broad in the middle of it all was Nicholas Jones with some unfortunate student propped before him, rustling frantically through a ragged backpack for what could only be a hastily written excuse proffered by the boy's parents. It was surely, by now, so long overdue that it couldn't matter—Deputy Jones is a stickler for the minutiae of regulation, you see. And committed to a doctrine of minor humiliation to boot.

The boy's peers broke either side of him, meandering away from Jones's man-made obstruction of the corridor. Heads went down, eyes were averted. Nobody wanted Mr. Jones to suddenly remember some intricate and missing detail about them...

My problem with Jones, incidentally, apart from an acute dislike of the man, is his method. It's ham-fisted. It's a shove where a push would do. Effective in the majority of cases and therefore erroneously held up as successful. But its success lies in the fact that most students are compliant in the first instance and what we find then, in those rare circumstances where a student resists authority, is that Jones's heavy-handed tactics only serve to escalate the problem. But Jones would be apoplectic at any suggestion of mediation. A word in the ear, to him, is tantamount to surrender. He's a low-level tyrant, you see, and his belief in discipline is as crude as it is fundamental. He values discipline more than he does people, in fact. He has no faith in us at all...

Like the students, I spotted Jones ahead and put my eyes to the floor. I rounded him, at the depth of at least two bodies, and passed without the need for pleasantries. But Jones's comic obesity is never afraid to play on itself and I could sense his impending threat as he hurriedly concluded his interrogation of the student and bounded after me like an inflated slug.

'Al! Could I have a word?'

He clapped me heavily on the shoulder, craned his neck around, so that he looked into my eyes, as we walked the final ten feet of corridor, moving into the foyer and stopping at the door to the staffroom.

Fearing that if I entered the staffroom with Jones on my shoulder I might be stuck with him for twenty minutes, I stopped abruptly. I lifted my free hand to my head, as if suddenly and theatrically struck by a significant thought. 'Just hit me, Nick, I'm after leaving my poetry book in the classroom. I'll have to go back. Sorry, can I catch up with you again?' I said, turning and facing back down the corridor from where I'd come.

'It'll keep. But maybe you could think about something for me, could you?' he asked.

'Sure.'

'Simon Atley.'

'Yes? In my English class.' *Fuckwits, the both of you.*

'I saw you talking with him this morning. You having any problems with him? We need some ammunition to take to the board. You know what I mean?' ...

I was moved to side with the boy, actually, despite being sickened by the thought of the gangrenous leper, and without knowing what otiose rule he may have breached of late. Anything to oppose Jones, basically. That is how I set my moral compass ...

'And help in these processes never goes unnoticed. Long-term. Won't do you any harm. I can make sure of that,' he said.

'No problems with the boy on my side of things, Nick,' I said. *Unfortunately for you, you gobshite.*

'Right,' Jones said, 'I might come back to you on it though. And I'll keep you in mind, Al. Don't worry about that.'

In mind? For what?

I turned, immediately, and strode back down the by then deserted corridor. Jones, fat-browed with earnestness, stood for a moment before lumbering through into the foyer and accosting a student signing in late. *Prick!* I thought ...

Jones, of course, was at the heart of the only serious falling out of mine and Val's marriage. Another fine reason to detest the man. Sixteen months previously, it was, when upon hearing of the promotion of the younger, and considerably less competent, Nicholas Jones to the Deputy Headship, at a time in my career when it might have been assumed I would be wanting for more than the daily grind of the classroom, Val wondered whether I might have experienced regret at having not pursued the position myself.

The question inferred that I had become a disappointment to her, as far as I could see. But I couldn't understand how. At no point in our courtship or our marriage had I ever expressed interest in testing my mettle beyond the classroom. Ever. In fact, I had been explicit in my determination to see out my professional days in precisely the role I had entered it—as a teacher. I was adamant that if our marriage had all of sudden begun to manifest itself as failure, that it was on her head. If I, now on the cusp of half a century and amounting to no more than a *mere* teacher, had become a source of embarrassment to Val, among her sewing circle friends or coffee-morning gossips, well it was because she had changed.

My commitment to Val is elementary, you see. The promise, though not verbally declared so much as conveyed through a prevailing disposition over the course of a lifetime together, has always been the relative comfort of a teacher's salary; safe, reliable and unspectacular. If she has now come to resent that same modesty and wish for ambition in her easily contented husband—him being me—then it is her own demons that need reckoning. That's how I see it...

But anyway, as I was saying, it was just another inconspicuous evening in our house when Val launched this bolt across the table. I had, with a set of minuscule screwdrivers that I find infinite use for and pride far above any other functional item in the house, been undoing, disconnecting, refitting, testing and retesting a faulty smoke alarm. And I continued to take the smoke alarm apart, on a side plate, while my lamb—falling succulently from the bone—went steadily cold...

Purposely left to go cold; I'm no saint. I think it's only fair to say that. And Val's prize lamb is no joking matter. Not an issue to be fucked lightly with, I can assure you ...

So, yes, as I say, it was at this point, whilst straddling the satisfaction of her perfectly executed roast and the frustration of a mute and ungrateful husband, that she chose to put the boot in on the issue of my career's stagnation. She calculated the risks and thought she'd go for it, I suppose.

'So Nicky Jones wrangled his way to the Deputy Headship,' she said, her knife gliding through a tender strip of lamb.

I looked up, but not suddenly enough to catch her mischievous eye. *Nicky!* I thought. *What kind of perversion is this? Is this faux affectionate moniker intended to mock further my innocent association with the fucking slob?*

I slid the smallest screwdriver into its pristine pouch, and shuffled the two halves of the smoke alarm's plastic casing neatly together on the plate. As I lifted my knife and fork, I replied, 'That's right, yes.'

'And you never told me?'

'No reason to.' I hovered maliciously over the lamb before spiking a small potato instead.

'But you don't like him much, do you?'

'No.'

'So it must have upset you? Annoyed you a little?'

'Why should it? His business.'

'Oh, Albert, come on. Are you telling me that it doesn't bother you that Nicky Jones, twelve years your junior, fat and belligerent as he is, is now effectively your line-manager? Please!'

'He's my nothing, Val. I teach my lessons and I mind my own business. And he's covering a career-break, I might add. It'll most likely be a position he sits in for a few years and amounts to nothing in the end. But if he wants to pursue a career in administration, good luck to him.'

'Well, this is my point, Albert. You think you're better than him. You think he's a fool.'

'And I'm correct.'

'Well that fool is earning more money than you, and will be held in greater regard than you simply by rising higher. In twenty years' time your name won't be on any wall in that school and he'll probably be running it.'

'What do you want me to say, Val?'

'Don't you have even a trace of regret about not throwing your hat in the ring?'

I glared at her.

Sensing, perhaps, the territory she had entered, Val withdrew. 'I just wouldn't like to think you were bottling up any resentment, Al. You've made your choices, I know that. And you've made them for your own very good reasons.'

I pushed my plate away, lamb untouched. 'I'm not that hungry. I'll throw on a pizza or something later.' The ultimate dig.

There had never been cause for us to needle each other to life over dinner. Dinnertime banter had always alighted easily in our house, when the kids had still been at home. It was when Val's irrepressible interest in them was given free rein. And while enquiry and advice had bounced triangularly between her and them, my reclusive silence had been less evident, I suppose. I interjected only when I had something meaningful to say, while they seemed to speak just to indulge the fluctuating pleasurableness of each other's voices—conveying joy, fear and the gamut of in-betweens, without ever really saying anything much at all…

I like to speak but not to talk. That is one of Val's great dictums. Talking is what other people do. And as far as she is concerned it's a social failure of mine that I cannot conduct mundane conversation. There's a grain of truth to what she says, I expect, but I tell her that it's a great pity she hadn't been cute enough to make this subtle distinction before we promised our lives to each other.

'It's just an observation though,' she usually responds. She still loves me, after all. She says.

And I still love her. I do. Whether it's a criticism or an observation. We should be clear on that… But as far as family dinners go, the dynamic in our house suited me just fine. I liked to hear the children's voices, as if from a distance, and to know they were there and life was good for them, but my mind has always been someplace else. Living in a haze, imagining greater selves that I might have been; that I would be. I'd nod, hem and haw, and occasionally ask questions or laugh engagingly, but I was elsewhere...

But, but, but, but - there seem a lot of them now, don't there? Qualifying everything I say. Making excuses for myself. Already. At this early stage...

No matter. I'll continue...

Laughter, when it came, was most likely to be in response to something Abi deigned to share. That's fair to say. This realisation was slow for Val but once Abi left for college it became unignorable. Abi didn't exactly bring me out of my shell, but she got more blood from my reticent stone than most. I adore her. Always have.

In fact, there were long tracts of my marriage when the only conversations I felt I could bear were those with Abi; with my daughter, not my wife. This, I'm sure, though I'm not in the habit of commenting on how other people lead their emotional lives, is an unusual alliance. I don't wholly understand it but Abi is something other among the unremarkable rest. And what really draws me to her is that there has always been a strange sameness to her, from the first sight of her broadly rounded, crepuscular eyes. They stared back at me from within her shrivelled new-born frown, and took hold of me. From then on, I longed to be showered beneath the random drops of her flighty thoughts and hear the musical whims of her misplaced emphases. There was delight in her that caused me to thrust myself fatally down upon my own inadequacy. I fumbled over niceties and found the kind of mundane interest in her that I generally found insufferable in others...

I love the boy too, of course, but perhaps not the way I once did. I must say this, regrettably. Honesty is imperative, you understand. Jake was our firstborn and the experience reinvented me. We were very close and enjoyed each other's company in the earliest days. And the simple beauty of those memories still thrill me. They move me. Sincerely. But Jake grew up and out and into his own self, and by the time Abi was two or three, I had begun to withdraw. I don't know why, exactly, but it was certainly my doing.

Not his. And, as I say, I regret it...

In his own innocent way Jake might have been the only one who realised something had changed in me, I think. Maybe it was that insight, that feeling he had for what moved inside me that made me withdraw from him. Afraid of what cruelties I would show him. To protect him, even though his child's mind could never possibly interpret it as such, I hid from him. He knew me, felt the change in his very core, long before anyone else got a sniff of it. Decades before. Part of my soul was strangely adrift, you see, and my capacity for life was a deteriorating force...

But to return to the matter at hand: my point is this—the relatively easy flow of words between Abi and I obscured the failures of my other relationships, and allowed me, by and large, to go near on twenty years without speaking much to anyone. There were times when I'd speak a few words at the dinner table and find that my own voice seemed to catch me by surprise, to the extent that I'd quickly shut up. It was odd, I knew, that a man who spent his whole working life projecting his voice through acoustically impoverished spaces should find the sound of his own voice so arresting. But I did.

It was some strange combination of all these factors that made Val's comment on the Deputy Headship so incendiary, and even though in the world history of fallouts it wouldn't register, it was enough for us to not talk for a few days after. To dine alone each of those subsequent nights...

Lunch times at school are tiresome. Usually I sit alone. In a battered armchair, eating from my lap, with a coffee on the floor beside me. I am sworn to nothing but a fruit cup for lunch. I attribute my leanness to it, as well as my intellectual alertness. One hundred sit-ups every evening before my shower and a fruit cup for lunch. That's the programme, except on weekends, when I spoil myself with a homemade smoothie...

Routine is central. To everything. If there's one piece of advice I can offer, it is that. There are no guarantees in life, of course, but a sound routine achieves more than talk, hope, and inspiration ever will...

But yesterday afternoon, planted as I was in my favoured armchair, I watched with great discomfort as Aimeé Quinn and two car-fulls of other staff grabbed wallets and handbags and made their way out the door to an impromptu staff lunch. The gluttony and the collegiality of these little culinary excursions appal me, I may as well say. The latter, incidentally, I regard as the nadir of professionalism; sickening management-speak. But I've always forgiven Aimeé her part in this nonsense on account of her near-perfection.

I am well-practised at keeping my counsel. Just sucking things up. I've had to be. But yesterday afternoon, just as I forked a lush cube of melon, Nicholas Jones placed his hand on Aimeé Quinn's arm...

I almost choked. It was like a serrated knife to the fucking guts, if you must know...

Then he opened the door and held it for her. And she accepted the courtesy graciously, laughing back at some absurdity he'd thrown her.

I rocked myself from the depth of the armchair and onto my feet, fruit cup in hand. I left my lunch down and crossed toward the door of the staffroom. From the foyer, I peered after them. They broke from each other and walked either side of his car. My shoulders and chest tightened. Without a clear thought as to how the scene might unfold, I placed my hand on the door handle and prepared to pursue them; one of them. I wasn't sure which one. A wounded vocalisation broke within me and I was set to bellow unrepentantly across the forecourt, when they were joined by another colleague. It caused me to stand firm and watch. As they climbed into Jones's car, he already in the driver seat, I observed Aimeé looking to her colleague, who was clearly giving her a bit of a ribbing for her uncomfortable frolic with the fat bastard, and her innocence was proclaimed by ridiculing eyebrows to the heavens and a delectable titter.

I almost folded into my feet like a paper slinky. The sweet relief. I exhaled. There was nothing between them...

The afternoon brought two lessons. In the first I played the avuncular scholar, introducing a simple extract, procuring the limited responses from a range of young pupils and praising everybody's effort equally. A standard lesson acted out so many times before. I was barely conscious for its duration.

The second required more concentration.

'Abbott.'

'Sir.'

'Atkins.'

'Sir.'

'Atley… Yes, Mr. Atley. Indeed. Any sign of that essay you owe me?'

'End of the week, Sir. Definitely.'

'I may be your only friend right now, Mr. Atley. Don't abuse my leniency. This is a final final deadline. You understand?'

'I do, Sir. Thanks, you've been very decent about the whole thing,' he said, I recall.

Aside from the minor irritation of the boy, the rest was uneventful. I delivered a master class—relative to second level education, that is—in the tragic significance of Jay Gatsby: *So what is it, lads and ladies, that we can say about Jay Gatsby, James Gatz, The Great Gatsby!? He's an illusion, neither true to himself nor the world. In becoming something other, he loses himself. The person he desires to be is shallow, immoral, corrupt, because his dream is money. His great act is wealth. He thinks his dream is Daisy, is love; but Daisy is money. It jingles in her voice, a voice bereft of loyalty and decency. Money in The Great Gatsby both corrupts and is corrupt. The New York of the roaring 1920s, Jazz and decadence and boorishness, and intimate carelessness, is the holy alter of capitalism, and the old money of East Egg are the high priests. Gatsby fawns over their vast wealth, even as he resents them. They reward his ambivalence by sacrificing him. They tear his heart out like some ancient necromancer, holding the still-beating muscle in their closed fist, as the guilty blood of excess streams down their arms. Then they scurry off with blood on their hands and their souls vacant. They live, he dies. The rich enjoy the spoils while the poor pay the bill. The tragedy of James Gatz! A man who in all his moral failures somehow stands tall above the other characters in the novel. And then we get the sting in the tail – the unreliable narrator. Just as we arrive at our safe conclusion, we ask ourselves—Can we trust the story we've been told? The narrator is compromised. Does this change the conclusion or bolster it? Who can say? You can, my scholars. Make an argument, take part. Assume your views. Go forth and criticise!'*

Along those lines, at least. You know. An impassioned summation of the term's work. Bog standard in many ways but casually inspirational in others. I mean to their lives. Where else would they find this kind of thing? That's what I've always told myself. Puts some of them on the road to betterment, hopefully. We can't save them all, of course. Not even most of them. But we might just catch the attention of the next Einstein, Hawkins, Yeats, Beckett. You know. You never can tell which seeds will ultimately take. But this is our legacy, our footprint upon the world ...

Witness Interview 1.
Simon Atley, 17, student

I saw Sir that morning, yeah.

Seemed okay.

I asked for an extension.

He was annoyed but okayed it, yeah

Never talked much to you anyway, you know the way. He'd be walking away from you.

Next time I saw him? Last period. The afternoon. Asked me for the essay. There was no way I'd have been having it. Not that quick. End of the week he said.

He was a bit weird about it, now that you say. Said he wanted to be my friend or something. A bit queer, you know. Rattled me, to be fair.

Listen, I just told him I'd have it end of the week.

Shut up shop. Head down, you know. Didn't want him droppin' the hand or nothing.

Then? Jesus, eh, not sure… Oh, yeah, he went off on one. Complete fucking detour. Tangent central! Mumbling and muttering. Couldn't make head or tail out of it now. Talking to the roof he was. Head in the air. All the bullshit about the book, you know. Money corrupting people. The girl being a prostitute or something. I mean, I read bits of that book and I never saw anything about that. Off-The-Fucking-Wall!

After that? Wrote a question on the board. His hands were all inky. That's another thing actually. The ink, yeah. He was like a bit OCD about the classroom being clean and everything. The inky hands. And he was scrubbing them at the sink for ages. Usually he'd be at you for doing nothing, you know, but he just let us be. Nobody was talking or nothing, now, but he left us at it.

31

Just sat at his desk.

Was writing something. Kept rubbing the hands. All Lady Mac and all, you know.

Bell went. We waited. He could be a real bollocks now if you jumped before he said so, you know. You'd be sitting in till half-four some days. If you jumped up. But he didn't say anything, so we left.

He's grand, in a way. Not the worst of them. Bit of an oddball.

Stranger than usual that day? Couldn't say. Maybe, yeah. But later... now that's a whole other story. Off-The-Fucking-Wall! One hundred percent. Mental.

Two

… I was still on the school premises when Val rang. *What now, Val? For the love of Jesus!* 'Yes, dear?'

'Al, just reminding you about my appointment,' she said. 'You know I won't be back till late, right? But I'll pick up something for dinner. Just reminding you. I wasn't sure you were listening this morning.'

'Okay, Val. Sure.' *I'd written you out of the equation for the entire evening, if you must know.*

'Maybe have something small when you get in—a few crackers and cheese, maybe. But don't fill up and have me wasting dinner,' she said…

This was the level of conversation we had been reduced to, you see. Depressing. Truly depressing…

'Sure, Val. Thanks for the concern.' *I'm not six fucking years old!*

'No need to get defensive, Al. I didn't mean anything by it. I just don't want to be throwing food out because you've capitulated under absentmindedness again.'

'Okay, Val. I think I've got it now.' *Eat small, don't ruin dinner. Be a good boy.*

'See you later, sweetheart. Love you.'

'Sure, yeah. See you later.'

She remained on the line and I held the handset to my ear, confused as to what else might need saying.

'Do you even remember what my appointment is, Al?' she finally asked.

'Doctor?'

'Obviously. But you haven't even asked. It could be serious.'

'Is it?'

'No! But that's not the point, is it?'

I'm not sure, Val. Seems like it might be.

'Try listening to me, Al, would you? Please. Talking with me once in a while,' she pleaded.

But I'd had enough. 'I will, I will.' *And you can try being mute, Val.*

The end of the school day had rung-out three quarters of an hour by the time I'd tidied my desk and walked the abandoned upper corridor. The voices of lingering students, hurrying staff, and the small cleaning crew could be heard echoing from below, at the bottom of the hard-shined staircase. I passed through it all without a word or a nod; unnoticed among the clangouring triangulation of agendas, slipping like a wraith between the shadows of the corridor and the voices, and entering into the bright foyer with a sense of having succeeded in an endeavour both empty and thrilling.

In the staffroom the photocopier still thrummed, turning out reams of notes and questions. Some were still sitting over the last teas and coffees of the day, talking shop, while others poured over texts in preparation for upcoming lessons, and the scratch and rustle of car keys swept from table tops, or hurried good-byes, sounded the end for those commuting teachers in a race against peak traffic; a phenomenon existing beyond the borders of the town.

But my attention was consumed by Aimeé Quinn, her ungraspable beauty smothering all discernible sights and sounds and replacing them with a vacant gaze and barely observable but distinctly guttural grunt, low in my throat...

I was sick with love. That's the truth of it...

I wondered how her lunch had been and what fun they'd partaken in at the expense of Nicholas Jones's pitiful flirtation? I wondered what she ate? Something sophisticated, no doubt. An imaginative leafy salad, maybe. A delicate fish-based dish. Nothing battered, fried, or doughy, anyway.

And then, suddenly, she was upon me, catching my eye and landing some flutter-light fingertips on my withered hand.

'Hi, Al. How're you?' she asked, sweeping by me.

Her peculiar smile, so filled with tiny imperfections, somehow made her even more alluring; the uneven lips, sometimes spongy and other times taut, a slightly crooked tooth among the bottom row, and her lithe tongue smouldering behind her teeth as she spoke.

She half-spun to hear my response but kept walking...

I could have licked her from head to toe...

'Good, Aimeé. You?'

'Great. See you tomorrow,' she said, making for the door.

Indeed, Aimeé. Tomorrow. And tomorrow and tomorrow.

'She's a fine little thing, isn't she?' I suddenly heard. Jones was standing beside me, gawping after her. 'Just broke-up with her boyfriend, I hear. On the grapevine. What do you reckon?'

'These things happen, Nick.' The must of beefy stew, or something like it, was on his breath. *You lecherous bastard!*

'What would you do, eh?' he whispered, eying up the last of Aimeé's strut to the door...

I could have puked!...

'She's a nice girl, alright,' I trotted out, as Aimeé disappeared safely away from his filthy attention.

'Nice?' Jones exclaimed. 'Nice is slippers and beer, Al. That's sex on a stick! On two sweet, succulent sticks.'

... Oh, the bile! Up to my fucking tonsils, I was! Nauseous with his perversions...

'Okay, Nick!' I broke in. 'Not having this conversation. It's not fair.'

'Oh, sorry, Al. Just messing about. If you were ten years younger... if you weren't happily married... if, if, if,' Jones mocked. 'Sure it would only be frustrating for a man of your age. I'm still barely young enough to get away with it myself, I suppose. Last throes of youthful bravado!'

Youthful? My age? Frustration? You repulsive slob! Didn't you just see what happened between us? I raged. *What failed to happen when you laid your smutty hand on her arm? Can't you see how she regards you? Can't you see... the connection. You corpulent fuck!*

'I think she's a good kid, okay, I like her.' I couldn't even look at her.

'I bet you do, you dirty old bastard,' he said, patting me on the back and moving away. 'Just teasing, Al.'

You son-of-a-bitch! Everything about you!

'By the way, have you turned up anything on Atley yet?'

A fitful rage blew across me, and with my focus shot I had to leave. I needed to be free of the school, of the business of Nicholas Jones. I couldn't believe the vile mouth on the man. And poor Aimeé. Going about her day as if everything was sweet and good with the world. How little she knew of it...

Witness Interview 2.
Nicholas Jones, 36, Deputy Head

I SPOKE WITH ALBERT twice that day. The first time regarding a troublesome student whose attendance and behaviour record were due before the Board of Management. The boy was a serial truant. And when he was present his behaviour was alarming. I'd rather not name names or cite specific incidences but ultimately the boy's expulsion was a Health and Safety matter.

Oh, he'll be protected by a pseudonym, will he? Still, I'd prefer just to call him *the boy*. I'll try and keep this on as professional a footing as possible, if you don't mind. Gossip and rumour are things I try to steer clear of.

He was a danger to himself and others, the boy. Albert taught him and I'd seen them in conversation that morning. At the steps of the teachers' entrance. It struck me as inappropriate. To approach a teacher there, like that. Virtually accosting Albert. That prompted me to consult with Albert. He mentioned a few issues he'd had with the boy earlier in the academic year. He'd recorded them and was going to pass them along, he assured me. Unfortunately, for now obvious reasons, Albert never got round to that. But the boy's case got its hearing before the Board, and in the end the absence of Albert's documentation—the regrettable and tragic absence—proved immaterial.

The second meeting? End of the day. The staffroom, I recall. He seemed a bit distracted.

I approached him. As a friend, really. He seemed unusually concerned for one of our colleagues. She'd been having a hard time of it. Albert was upset. And distracted. I enquired after them both. He got very... how should I put this... defensive. So I changed the subject. I asked again about our troublesome student and the information he'd promised me. He said he didn't have it to hand. And we haven't spoken since, sadly. Again, for obvious reasons.

People have asked me did I notice anything unusual? And I've asked myself that too. At the time, yes, there was something that didn't seem quite right. But could I say that, looking back, we should have known that he was headed right in off the deep-end? No, I don't think so. I thought maybe he was a bit disaffected. Or lovesick.

Lovesick? Oh, I don't know really. Hard to say. That's just a thing that came to mind, at the time. That afternoon. The way he stood, or looked, maybe. Or spoke, perhaps. I'm sure there's nothing in it. Just an impression.

He was an odd fish, Albert. Kept to himself, mostly. He was my mentor when I first arrived at the school, actually. And we had a great regard for each other, professionally. I don't know what could have come over him, frankly. Val was a lovely woman. She deserved better than... I don't know. Can I say *madman*? Is that not very PC? Do we know? Was he actually... is he... insane? Or has a motive been discovered? Something illicit? It doesn't seem like the Albert we all know, or thought we knew. But until it's ruled out I suppose everything is in the mix, isn't it?

Come back to me again, if needs be. Whatever I can do. Come back to me. Feel free. By all means.

Three

... At Handy's Hardware, on the far end of town, I realised I had walked out of the school without my jacket and satchel. I would not go back though. The place and its people sickened me.

I examined the disorderly display in the window; a shovel, a pitchfork, a hoe, a plough, a petrol mower and a strimmer, a pruning shears, a pruning saw, an axe, a mattock, a leaf blower, a hedge trimmer, a rake, a rotary tiller, a lopper, an eighty metre hose, and the basics, like gloves and a watering can. All sorts. But Jones's sleazy hand and how it had been laid upon Aimeé's arm wouldn't leave me alone. I couldn't shake it. His sleazy hand. Her arm. Uninvited.

'Evening, Mr. Jackson. How're you?'

Dave Handy was a pupil of mine. Twenty years ago nearly, it struck me as I turned to greet him. He'd been academically weak but tremendously honest in his endeavour. His parents had fretted about his schooling, not knowing enough to help him themselves but worried sick by his mediocrity; so devout were they in their belief in the emancipating powers of education. But as a teacher I had recognised, as had most anybody who knew Dave Handy, and probably Handy himself, that where he was headed was the family business. His parents, well-meaning and engaged as they were, wanted more for their son, without realising that he had just about all he wanted right there in town. What had been admirable in Dave Handy was that the knowledge that his schooling would prove all but irrelevant never prevented him from working to the nth degree of his potential. His diligent decency became the stuff of legend. That decency, that endearing honesty, has been embellished over time so that now he is that thing all pleasant but transient experiences become—a sentimental giant.

A myth, a glorious untruth that virtue is measured against forever more. What is admirable in any student has become synonymous with Dave Handy: 'He's got a bit of Dave Handy about him, that one,' someone will say; or, 'If only that crowd had a Dave Handy or two among their ranks.'

'Anything I can help you with?' he asked, leaning against the wall, smoking.

'Maybe, David. My pruning saw is busted. Overgrowth.' *Got some big, fat, obnoxious overgrowth that needs cutting back.* 'So I need a strong one.'

'Trees or heavy shrubbery?

'Both really.'

'Come on in then. I'll sort you out,' Handy said, finishing his cigarette and flicking it onto the road. 'And how's everything up at the school these days, Sir?'

I looked about and entered the shop, not exactly missing the question, simply allowing it to sail by me; an uncharted comet across a fantastical sky. 'And some rope. And that shovel,' I said, pointing at the shovel in the window display.

I patted my trouser pockets as Handy gathered the items. I had no cash and realised that my house keys too must have been still at school, in my bag or jacket. But still I wouldn't go back. My bank card was tucked in behind the cover of my phone and that was all I needed.

Ten minutes later I took up a seat at a table on the street outside Terri Carlson's. I sat alone, my new pruning saw, shovel and five metre length of rope assembled about me, and avoided unnecessary interaction.

Over coffee, I tried to work loose threads of what had been troubling me into a single narrative strand: the apprenticeship served by Nicholas Jones under my keen tutelage; how Jones's precocious rise to management had betrayed all I'd taken the time to teach him; the implications of Val's historical observations regarding my professional stagnancy; Jones's sudden interest in my most wayward student; Jones's unsolicited offer of support for an ambition he imagined, as Val did, resided somewhere within me; Jones's sniffing around Aimeé Quinn; Jones's dismissal of me on the ludicrous grounds of my vintage.

I scribbled these musings onto a notepad borrowed from the boy who had served me, trying to draw credible fact from the tenuous. Tracing over and over phrases that satisfied the ego. Etching them into existence ...

It's a habit I formed while in college, in fact, when I religiously kept a journal. In many respects the thoughts in my journal are more real to me than the actual daily events of my life. There is more of me between the lines. But it is a habit that I have fallen out of, unfortunately, although in times of turmoil I often resort to pen and paper and introspection as a means of purging emotional tension. I write it out of me on a loose sheaf of paper, read it over a few times, tear it up and move on ...

The afternoon was pushing into early evening by the time I brought the abstracted musings to a cold conclusion. I sat deathly still and watched as the town spluttered to a standstill: traffic thinning to a shady tail on main street; workers and shoppers getting on the road home; shopkeepers signalling the close of business with partially lowered shutters and the sandy scratch of yard brushes on the paths.

The tables either side of me had chairs on top of them and the evening was in lush descent, when, at my feet, out of nowhere, there was an adolescent boy with a brush, flicking scraps and crumbs into a pan. 'I'm just about finished,' I said.

But the boy didn't even acknowledge I'd spoken.

I glowered at him; his mohawked scalp, his insolent back ...

The curvature of the contemporary spine, incidentally, causes me peculiar offence. Slobbish, tasteless, lazy. No posture ...

'Hey,' I said, forcefully nudging the boy's ribs with my foot. *I'm talking to you, you cheeky fuck!*

The boy stood up and removed an earphone from one ear. 'What's that?'

'I said I'm just done here. Sorry to hold you up.'

'No bother,' he said, placing his earphone back in his ear. Plugging the hole to the outside world. Insulating himself with the clang and screech and thump of music that sang distinctly of his vacuous generation.

I didn't recognise him. Which probably meant he attended what we call with great and just superciliousness, 'the new school.' The community college, opened ten years ago on a large greenfield site well outside of town, and decked out with every piece of technology conceivable, but never embraced as part of the town proper. Built as the town has sprawled slowly outward, it has become a kind of floating institution, a satellite building to house those who are officially but not really part of the town. Never truly accepted, its residents, who have settled only in the last decade, are interlopers really. 'The new school' is an extension of their world; a sterile imposter, characterless and devoid of any discernible ethos or culture.

In this sense, the boy's rudeness and social ineptitude were consistent with his place in the town. So I swept the coffee mug from the table and sent it to splinters on the path outside the shop. Then I stood up, tucked in my shirt, chest and jaw protruding, and stared defiantly at the boy. *Let that be a fucking lesson to you!*

I took up the pruning saw, shovel and rope, and set off for home. Behind me, Terri was hugging and kissing somebody goodbye on the pavement. She said, 'See you soon, Al,' as I walked away. 'Say hello to Val for me.'

'Will do, Terri,' I replied. *But don't expect my patronage to continue with customer service of this ilk!...*

Witness Interview 3.
Terri Carlson, 46, Shopkeeper

IT WASN'T STRANGE AT ALL for Al to stop in for coffee. Especially in the months recent to that. And it was a beautiful evening, I tell you. And we were busy. Right up till shutters-down. A lot of folk stopped in and just watched the evening settle.

He'd dropped in that morning too, yes. But we barely spoke. Ordered his usual. Big line behind him. There were the usual pleasantries. Entirely ordinary.

With hindsight... the garden tools... what's the word? Ominous, yeah. Saw and a shovel. But Al was known to do the odd bit of garden work. My Jim would've seen him out manys an evening, still in his suit trousers and the ends tucked into some old hobnails. We used to laugh at it. But now—Jesus, had I known.

I didn't notice any rope. Not saying it wasn't there. Just saying I didn't notice it.

Val was an awful nice lady actually. And Al too, for that matter. He was good fun in his own way. And a good teacher, that's what my kids will tell you. I mean, I heard about the town that he'd gone a bit off the wall towards the end. Some of that's probably just gossip though, fitted to the rumours after the fact. But it's an angle that's out there now, that's for sure.

I feel sorry for him in a way. Sorrier for Val, obviously. Poor, poor Val. And the kids. By God, the poor kids! They're nice enough, you know. The boy could be a little arrogant, sometimes. Like Al, I suppose. But Al seemed to carry it in a softer way. The girl? She was sweet as pie, to be honest. A clever one too.

No, I've nothing else to add. Except—give them their privacy. Don't you think?

Four

... I ARRIVED ON THE GRAVELLED driveway of our home, still fuming, with the rope hanging like a bandoleer over my shoulder and across my chest. In one hand the shovel was swinging and in the other the pruning saw. Only then, on the porch, did I set about wondering how I would get in without keys. I scaled the side-gate and checked round the back of the house for an open window. I checked in the usual places for a key left out, already knowing I'd find nothing; in domestic affairs, forethought and precaution are my brief and I knew I'd not left out a spare key.

So I committed to breaking a window and was only slowed by considering which windows would grant easiest access, which ones would cost least to replace and which one would be least conspicuous; an argument with Val was not on my agenda for the evening.

That's not how I want this to end, I said, standing before the front door.

The final decision did not satisfy all of the criteria but ultimately I had little choice. I put the handle of the shovel through the smallest pane of glass on the front door, hollowing it out as completely as I could. Then I reached in and around to the latch. It clicked and the door opened.

As I withdrew, the jagged tooth of some remaining glass in the frame tore through the sleeve of my shirt and the skin on the underside of my forearm. I winced. The blood came fast down my frayed shirt sleeve. Thrusting my hand in the air, like that boy from the Frost poem, I clasped the injured arm with my other hand. It was necessary to let it go for an instant so that I could knock off the alarm, but then I made for the kitchen.

The wound was only superficial, despite the melodrama of its quickened bleeding, and I soon had it cleaned and lightly bandaged. I stripped off my shirt, torn and bloodstained, and dropped it in the kitchen bin. The cool air on my bare chest was liberating but in the reflection of the sliding glass doors I was mortified to catch sight of a seal of flabby fat oozing above my belt-tightened waistline, and falling over the top of my trousers. *It is right,* I told myself, *that I am disgusted. What chance have I of self-betterment if I cannot acknowledge my own repulsiveness?* The sudden thought of Aimeé Quinn, the hopelessness of me and her, twisted in my gut and I covered myself with a T-shirt pulled from the clothes-horse...

The next thing I recall was my phone vibrating:

VAL: DLAYED AT DOCS. HOME SOON AS. N JONES IN WAITING ROOM! TELL U LATER! X

I snapped shut the cover of my phone and slid it across the counter, away from me. From beneath a mound of ice creams, frozen vegetables and leftover meals in the freezer, held onto in a domestic pantomime of frugality, I unearthed a pizza.

I laid out the new pruning saw and the length of rope on the kitchen table, the shovel against a chair and took a seat. I had just poured a large rum and mixer, when the doorbell rang.

'Mr. Jackson?' a woman's voice called in from the hallway.

'Of course,' I responded, coming out from the kitchen and finding a police officer spying through the window frame I'd chiselled out.

I opened the door and parked myself across the threshold.

'We've had a call from a neighbour. Is everything alright here?' she asked, surveying the glassless frame in the door and the broken glass still on the doormat.

'Oh, yes. Lost my keys,' I said, raising eyes at my own incompetence. 'My wife's at the doctors and wasn't going to be back. It's been a long day. Foolish, I know. And it'll cost me in the end, of course.' *Impulsiveness always does.*

'Breaking into your own house isn't a great idea, Mr. Jackson.'

'Oh, listen, I know. And I apologise for any waste of your time, but everything is fine here.'

A second officer stepped from the car at the gates. 'Everything okay there, Denise?' he called over.

I recognised the face just as it recognised me.

The second officer closed the door of the car and walked toward us. 'Mr. Jackson, how're you?' he asked at the doorstep. 'Everything okay here?'

'Yes, it is. I know your face, sorry, but the name…'

'I'm a few years gone now. One of thousands. Anthony Tallis,' he said, reaching out his hand. 'Nice to see you again.'

'Yes, Anthony. Nice to see you too,' I said.

'What happened to the window?'

'I was just telling your colleague here. Stupid thing to do. Forgot my keys. Had a bit of a day. Was a little rash. I apologise. Don't want to waste anyone's time.'

'But everything's okay?' officer Tallis asked.

'Yes, Anthony. Thanks.'

'Your wife home?' the other officer asked.

'No, she's not. At the doctors, as I said.'

'Okay, Mr. Jackson, Sir. You sure everything's okay?' Tallis asked, glancing casually about.

'Yes. All fine now.'

'Fair enough,' he said, tapping his partner on the back.

She stood planted to the spot, looking past me down the hall, and about the porch. Tallis moved off and eventually she began to move with him.

'Dinner's just ready actually,' I said, signalling over my shoulder. 'Do you mind?'

'Not at all. See you again,' Tallis said, as he reached the gate.

His partner moved more slowly and shifted her gaze about the front garden with reserved suspicion, a face shrivelled and curled in on itself like a walnut.

I waved them off and closed the door…

My weapons were laid out before me, like a man of war, and I felt comfortable in their lethal presence. Comfortable enough to eat and read, in fact.

Having eaten three slices of pizza and nearing the bottom of my second rum, while immersed in a chapter of Dostoevsky, re-reading it in parts for the first time in decades, I became exhilarated by the unnerving parallels between Raskolnikov and me: the call to vulgarity by a higher purpose, for example, and a certain superiority.

At intervals I stopped reading and lapsed into highfalutin oration, rehearsing monologues for my enthralled audience—the inanimate weapons. I was almost apologetic, at times, with regard to the arrogance of my story, but argued, in response to the astute and erudite questions from the attending arsenal, that any assumed arrogance was inextricably linked to actual superiority, and therefore rendered it forgivable. Such frankness, I acknowledged, could be difficult for people to take. *We're not accustomed to such candidness. Such honesty. Are we?* I put to them.

There was great pleasure in this evening stretch. In this escapism. Sitting alone in the kitchen, just reading and conversing with myself. It helped, of course, that my appetite had been placated and the slow fuzz of two large rums was humming in my head. And, of course, what heightened my appreciation of the moment was the memory of how things had once been. While the children had still been children, you understand. For over twenty years, the bulk of my adult life, the TV dominated the downstairs rooms, so that even when I muted it because they weren't really watching—though never did I dare to turn it off for fear of having to engage in debate or discussion and so losing more time in the process—the constant monotony of it, forever in the background, despoiled my wish for a stimulus-free environment. It's a form of obsessiveness, I readily acknowledge—a compulsive sort—where my very being demands symmetrical tidiness and virtual soundlessness before a coherent thought can be spawned. I had always assumed that the children were the obstacle, and on that basis had surrendered to twenty years of life about the house, comfortable in the knowledge that the obstacle in question would one day up and leave us…

But, as I've said, it transpired that it wasn't the children, it was people. All people. And Val—my dear good wife, the woman I chose to spend my life with—well, it turns out she was both a person in her own right and the reason why others constantly

infringed upon my longed for quietude. I mean, if it wasn't her
and her damn radio it was the never-ending phone calls, con-
ducted, without fail, while sitting in the same room, irrespective
of their intimate details. Or her volunteering of our kitchen as
a staging post for the monthly Residents' Association meetings.
And, god forbid, if silence did actually achieve itself, she was
compelled to disband it with questions, and affectionate touches,
and all the abhorrence of a cosy marriage.

So pizza, rum, and a book really were an event; a celebration
deserving of celebration itself. Evenings like this were sacred
and... precisely why Val was expendable, I suppose. More than
expendable; a cancer at the heart of purity. The pound closest to
the heart. To be cut out; excised and expunged.

Without her, potential stretched out in all directions: the
chance to be better; the opportunity to think more profoundly;
to be sexually available; to be private; to do as I please; to eat
or not eat; to read; to travel; to be the man I'd intended but
never spoken of; to be revered; to live again beyond the leeching
shadow of obligation...

Amidst these thoughts the searing electronic warble of a ringtone
ripped into the air. The house phone, on the hall table, can never be
ignored. It takes forty-five seconds to ring out and is jammed at the
loudest setting. You might see one call out, but if the person on the
other end is determined, they'll get you on the second.

I lifted the handset. 'Hello. Jacksons.'

'Hi, Dad. How're you?'

'Oh, Jake. Fine. And you?'

'Good. Is Mum there?'

'No, actually. Doctor's appointment.'

'Is something wrong?' he asked.

'I don't think so, no.'

'Right. Any news?'

*Besides your mother's betrayal of me? Or my colleagues ostracising
me? Or the fact that I've become something repulsive, more repulsive
even than I am pathetic?* 'Not much really. Same old, same old.
How about you?'

'Not much. It's just... I've inadvertently promised this girl a cooked meal. I thought Mum might help.'

'Is she a girlfriend, this girl?' I asked, before realising the answer didn't interest me.

'She's a friend. It's all fluid enough.'

'Right,' I said, envying him his young years.

'So no news, Dad? No? Just at home enjoying an evening alone? You should have been a hermit instead of a teacher.'

'Maybe.'

'I hear that shifty bollocks Jones is still balls deep in the Deputy Headship. Looks like they might make it permanent, by the sounds of things.'

'Your mother, no doubt?'

'Yeah. He's a shit though, isn't he?'

'As I have repeatedly told your mother, it's none of my business. I really don't care.'

'No interest yourself, no?'

'No.'

'Might freshen things up for you. Doing something different. A new challenge.'

'I'm a foot soldier, Jake. I want no more than that simple recognition.' *Either I've not got a big enough ego for it or I'm not self-sacrificing enough to devote myself to its banality. I can't figure which it is. But I do know I'm deficient in whatever qualities a manager is comprised of. I refuse to play their game. I'll not be complicit. Too much integrity on my end of things, quite simply.*

'You've got to move forward though, Dad. Got to find other things too. What'll you do, long-term, if you shut yourself away from everything? When that's gone, what happens? You'll drive yourself mad!'

'Yes, well ... I'll tell your mother you called.'

'Have you been talking with Abi at all?' he blurted out hurriedly.

'No.'

'I tried her over the weekend but we keep missing each other,' he said.

'Oh, yes, well that's unfortunate. Just life getting on with living, I suppose'

'Okay then, Dad. Talk to you again. Sorry if I've annoyed you. I didn't mean ...'

'It's fine. Bye.' *You ungrateful shit. Annoyed me? Too fucking right you have, sunshine! Sonshine? Laughable! ...*

Any remaining doubt in my mind found its origin in nostalgia. For when we had first known each other Val's effect had been to broaden and deepen, you see. Rather than suppress or imposition. To look at her now—in the end, I mean—would be to misrepresent her and what she was when we first met.

She was almost a woman then. And what a woman! I'm telling you! She had vigour and vitality. In her smart skirt and her sleek curves. Lean but full in the waist and chest. She carried herself on her toes in a precocious totter that defied the physics of her. Effortless. Unaware of her beauty. Unfazed by womanhood's infiltration of her body. That's what I thought when I saw her ...

But that kind of giddy abstruseness soared only momentarily before it choked in the thin air and disappeared into the smoky ceiling with the rest of my conceited ideas ...

For my own part, I was self-consciously underdressed, in a corduroy jacket worn over a marginally too small shirt, jeans and canvas trainers; entirely out of step with the decade. Only recently graduated as a teacher and already out of touch with the kids, she used to joke.

But none the less, it was there and as we were then, in the opulent glitter of a city bar, where the boorishness of bleached hair and grunge noisily competed with tarty lycra minis and fluorescence, that Val's understated blacks and creams, her sophisticated heel and just about respectable-length skirt, spoke differently to me. She seemed to know things others didn't ...

She was just different, you know. And, in essence, this is the quality that I find most attractive in anyone ...

So, there I was, with some tome, a European masterpiece, no doubt, lying akimbo on the bar as I rolled a few remaining peanuts to and fro under my hand, their coarse grain working against the calluses of my flattened palm. I added another butt to the ashtray and cast a discreet eye over her ...

A smoker back then, of course. Can hardly believe it myself, when I think of it. Filthy habit. Folly of youth, I suppose. Quit just before Jake was born. Stopped in a day. Just made a decision...

But I digress. Again. My apologies. Where was I...

Yes, I was resting my chin on the dipping knuckles of my interlocked hands, my head sunken to my shoulders, and peering over the froth at the top of my glass. I had already noticed her noticing me and turned my book back over and read a few more pages. Playing it cool.

In the interim between my awkward glances and unconvincing indifference, Val and her friends began their slow sidle down the bar towards me. Within an hour they were four women on one side of a right-angled corner and I was a single man on the other; a single man with a pounding heart, who feared that if these women actually talked to him that the sight of his tongue falling from his mouth, and hanging fat and limp from the back of his throat, would end the conversation before it ever got started.

'Do you mind?' Val's friend asked, plucking up the lighter I'd left on the bar top.

'Not at all,' I managed.

'Thanks. This is my friend, Valerie,' the friend replied, swinging Val by the elbow to face me.

This was the moment when I saw her most purely. Of course, in some sadly tragic way it was also the last time I ever would. And when we were first married, when Jake and Abi were still babies, I would recount for her how beautiful she appeared to me that night, and tell her that when I thought about her, about loving her, that it was that face I saw. I think the first time we see someone is in a way the only time we ever see them. Everything after is subject to distortion, isn't it?

Not something Val necessarily ascribes to, naturally, but her vastly underwhelmed response to this line of amateur philosophising has never stopped me. 'By association,' I add, or something like it. 'By experience and expectation.' But that first time it's pure, isn't it? As real as it gets. And in that pure moment

I saw inestimable beauty. Honestly, I looked at her and I saw something glowing. Sensual. A face of classical beauty. A fucking sculpture! That's what she was.

But that was before she was tarnished. By my clumsy affection. My blithering intimacy. But she's never got that, I don't think. And, of course, accustomed as she is to the unique deformity of my world's view—a view characterised by surging enthusiasm abruptly followed by plummeting qualification—she braces herself for imminent let down...

But then nothing I say is ever quite what I mean, you know the way? Disappointment, decay, is the inevitable conclusion to everything, I feel. That's sort of what I mean but it's not all of it either. Nothing endures, you know, and nothing ages as grotesquely as perfection. I was only ever trying to protect Val from that. It doesn't have to be a bad thing, that's what I wanted her to see...

Enough though! Enough! I know. Back to it. Back to the nearer present, which is what we're here for, isn't it...

After dinner, possessed by a compulsive need to make ready the perfect stage for my magnum opus, I found myself with my cheek plump on the hand-scraped hickory floor. Arms stretched out, crucified face-down.

I looked along the lines of the planks that ran through the living room and into the kitchen, as far as the sliding glass door. At the door, the dog panted, heavy-tongued and steamy with drool. A thick beam of sunlight cut through the glass at an angle across the kitchen floor. Particles drifted, dropped, and circled each other as the dog began to yelp, in search of my attention. In search of his master; the family dog...

As my stare bounced off the glass door and ran back toward me along the grainy visage of the floorboards, I noticed crumbs under the kitchen chairs and, close to my nose, some smudges in the dark knots of wood. Two lanes of floorboard above my nose, and only available to my upper-peripheral vision, bubbles rose through the rum and coke, dark as the wood it rested upon. I tilted my head to examine it, its murky hue transforming the row of books behind into something faintly antique. Viewed through the burnt sienna prism of the rum and coke, the scene was imbued with a mysterious weight. It provided depth and gravitas, qualities that would otherwise have been implausible in the circumstances; me on the floor, face down, suit trousers tucked into my socks, an un-ironed polo shirt on my trunk, accompanied only by my fourth drink, a dustpan and brush, a cloth, and some floor-cleaning spray...

Life through a rum and coke lens; what could be more poignant...

On the floor, I returned to Aimeé Quinn and the conspiratorial forces of Val and Nicholas Jones. I wondered if the situation was retrievable. I felt certain it was. *Aimeé will be impressed, for starters*, I said...

By my widower's resilience. Awed even. Once she sees how I handle life alone. And her comfort I'll quietly accept. We will grow close then, as a matter of circumstance; two colleagues, kindred spirits, enjoying the company of each other, until finally the humdrum of my middle-age subsides and gives way to reverence and desire. Her love for me will be an intuitive thing; grand and wise. Friends will commend me on her maturity and come to accept her not as Val's usurper but as an appendage of my indomitable happiness.

She is not yet anybody else's! I insisted to myself, emboldened rather than forewarned by her lampooning of Jones during the lunchtime debacle. *If she isn't his, she can still be mine. Stands to reason...*

In preparation for the rest of my life, a phrase that radiated with meaning, I began citing the failures of my relationship with Val. To closely examine the myths that constituted our marriage, and with clinical remove to charge those white deceits with intent to pervert the course of my fulfilment. But before I had time to wade too deeply into excessive self-pride, a knuckle tapped on the living room window. I rolled, like the dog would, one hundred and eighty degrees. Onto my back. With my knees and hands in the air, like four paws.

Val was peering in, with some difficulty it seemed, attempting to make sense of what her eyes presented. I lay strangely startled on the floor.

'What happened to the window, Al. What're you at?' she called out, as I approached down the hall.

'Cleaning the floor,' I said, plausibly enough.

'Cleaning the floor or thinking about cleaning the floor? And what's happened here? What about the window? I thought we'd been burgled.'

'Well, yeah, I haven't exactly started yet,' I said. 'And I was just about to clear up that glass,' I said...

I knew it would be the first thing she'd comment on and wondered why it hadn't been the very first thing I did upon coming home, irrespective of what cock-and-bull story I had concocted to explain it away...

Val walked down the hallway toward the kitchen and into the lingering aroma of pizza. I saw her shoulders stiffen. Her head shifting tensely, in search of some visual evidence to feed the burgeoning outrage; a sauce-stained plate, a dirty pizza wheel. She flung the two steaks onto the counter.

'Fucking hell!'

'I'll take the dog for a walk,' I cut in, grabbing the leather leash from the coat stand.

'I told you I was bringing dinner! I told you not to eat anything!'

'I forgot.'

She turned and looked at me, but I just rounded her while repeating the apology. I opened the sliding door and the dog scrambled in; the frictionless grate of long-nailed paws on the wood floor, frantic and desperate.

'Sorry,' I said. 'I forgot.'

After a moment, she sighed. 'Look, it's alright. But leave the dog till later, would you? At least sit down with me while I have mine.'

I was uncertain, suspecting this to be some form of entrapment, even though I knew Val needed company the way most people need love. As much as she laments my taciturnity, you see, she enjoyes my quiet company. Especially as she decants the events of the day. She finds tenderness in my ability to just nod along and say nothing, ignoring my blank-eyed stare, my repetitive stirring of the tea, or the way I trace the rim of a glass with my middle finger; always a middle finger and always with the other fingers dancing about it like a slightly manic flock of butterflies.

'The dog's hyper, Val. He needs a run.'

'Put him back in the garden, Al. Please. Have the decency to sit down with me. Let me tell you all about Nicky Jones. Oh, I'm telling you...'

The filthy bastard! Is he trying to fuck you too? 'I don't care about Deputy Jones, Val.' *He's a prize cock!*

'Oh, Al, but you'll like this. Wait till I tell you. He's such an asshole!'

Her partisan dismissal of the libidinous pervert almost redeemed her. But she was merely indulging me and I knew it. She wanted me at the table with her, sitting and listening.

I acquiesced and took my reluctant seat at the end of the table. She pulled out a pan and a chopping board. Two glugs of olive oil heated in the pan as she seasoned the two steaks with a pinch of salt and pepper. She took some leftover couscous from the fridge, diced some vegetables and tossed it all in a salad bowl. Her conversation ambled as she cooked, saving the juicy stuff for when she could concentrate properly on its delivery. Now that I'd submitted to it, the slandering of Nicholas Jones had me almost gloating, no longer bothered whether the dog was walked or not. But then Val put on the fan above the hob, roughing-up the relative tranquillity with its throaty rumble, and compounded the insult by turning on the radio.

With that my participation in the conversation, even in my most limited role as listener, ended...

Constant distraction, infantile attention span.

Conclusion: fear of silence. Of aloneness.

Net conclusion: irritation. For me.

This is what Val carries with her into our relationship. When we were younger I never noticed it. Now, however much I may wish it otherwise, I can only experience her through a conduit of insufferable traits. For decades you just don't see something, you

know, and then suddenly it's everywhere. All over you, grubby-
ing up your past, smothering your present and hampering any
future. And how momentously these tiny intolerances announce
themselves! It's fascinating, really, I think, that as people we do
this to each other. Get in the way of the other's happiness.

Just how irrepressible must our individuality be? When you
think about it. How powerful an instinct must our primary
selves possess that close to thirty years of human mastication,
grinding and kneading personal identities into near obscurity,
cannot yield harmoniousness? What an abject failure, what an
illusion, is human union? Why can't we simply love? Why does
our human affection carry with it an impulse to control? To
dilute the potency of its very focus?

Val no more loves my emotional absenteeism than I love
her nauseating neediness. We'd both gladly alter the other if we
could. There's no 'Wouldn't change a thing about you' mawkish-
ness to our relationship, you see. But to be fair, when we vowed
to take each other for better or worse, I'd wager that neither of
us considered that this was what we were talking about...

I have loved her, of course. I'm not saying I don't. But not
for her quirks of character. It's a primal force. It has to be. To
short-circuit what is congenitally individual in us. Anthropology
won't tell you this but as far as I'm concerned the role of a smart
wardrobe and nice heel in the cultivation of the contemporary
family unit has a lot to answer for, and it's a much neglected
field of study...

But that's another story, isn't it, and not the whole of it either,
not by a long shot...

But later, as Val and I grew entangled in each other, it was
the feel of her in my arms too. Or her smell, the natural and
the cosmetic. Sometimes, in the mornings, when she leaves a
light mist of perfume billowing behind her, I can almost feel her
again: the weight of her tender flesh, my palms cupped about it,
oozing between my fingers; and the taste of her, the distinctive
wetness of her lips and tongue. This is love, I think. A series of
effervescent sensations, beheld in the citadels of memory—smell,
taste, touch, sound, sight.

Love: the great illusion!

Because the things I love about Val no longer exist, you see. We're just two people who half know each other now, which is half better than anybody else, of course. But hardly the objective of matrimony. I know her well enough to know that all that we have in common is a distant affection, a sensation that is purely memory, a nostalgia whose joys and delusions fall further into dust with each passing heartbeat.

And what Val loves in me can be no more than memory either. But I know, for a fact, that she doesn't possess courage enough to ever admit that. So we're stuck. How simple is that? The best explanation I've devised yet; we're stuck ...

And my solution, the sticking plaster on the fatal wound? Dislocation ...

This is my cross to bear. I feel close to nobody. I am without allegiance. Without faith. Although I am capable of loving intensely, that is true. But it is always tainted by reservation. The one you love today, that loves you, may be lost in the caprices of how many tomorrows. That's inescapable. Not cynical.

There are things I still enjoy and people I love—in my heart of hearts I know there must be—but even in the midst of goodwill, or seasonal cheer, I am chronically unable to dismiss the nagging inconvenience of transience. That's my point. The inevitable and unavoidable recognition that no moment, no judgement, no experience is immune, has invoked emotional paralysis in me. Even as a young man, since my adolescence, the cardinal place of impermanence has caused me immense anxiety ...

And the associated disaffection of such enlightenment has had many random victims; the first among them was my dead grandmother, oddly enough. Collateral damage, let's call her, for I knew her only through the eyes of my boyhood self. And yet I still recall with odium her sudden descent into senility. And incontinence. Truly disgusting. I have never forgiven her for proving that the point of living is to die.

Whatever we learn of life, we learn it in death. At the death. That's for sure. She taught me that. The sheer pitilessness of that realisation shivered through me and shook me into a new disposition, a disposition that for all its newness was completely lacking in vitality. A teary kind of fatalism, it was. Persisting for years. Until I rose mighty with the vanity of mortal man and began a decade long railing against God. Not the man, the being, the deity himself, mind, because I'd long declared that a nonsense, but the concept and all its incarnations. I became vehemently irreligious, to an irrational extent, where I almost seemed to be blaming God for his failure to exist.

In the end I turned away from the family I had been born into too, having come to blame them when God couldn't be smoked out of his hole. I dismissed my parents as wholly and irredeemably insipid. But I was too drained by my decade warring with God to do anything but forget about them. I simply resolved to see as little of them as possible, blaming them for all measure of newly discovered and undesirable aspects of my being. I blamed them for haplessly allowing life to just happen, and for allowing it to happen to me. I blamed them for their religiosity and for not even bothering to be insulted by my ridiculing of their arcane faith. Why had they never shouted me down, challenged the manner in which I demeaned their quaint superstitions, their holy hocus-pocus, with the conviction of true believers? It was beyond me.

In time, I came to blame my parents for my apathy too, for a disposition that I obviously acquired from too many years spent with them. I'd inherited their listlessness and it left me empty. 'I realise now what I've been fighting all these years,' I finally told them one day, then in my late-twenties and a few years into my career. 'Christianity is a closed book. I can see that now. I accept my powerlessness. In the face of its pig ignorance, what other course is there? It doesn't desire to be opened or interpreted; a book that wants to stay on the shelf and just be accepted. And that's fine, but you should know that books that aren't read get forgotten. I want you to be clear on that. They disappear into oblivion. We all do. I'm sorry, truly, that we can't agree and that you can't respect my views, but that's the end of it. It's all I've got to say on the matter,' I said, sure that even as that rejection screeched past them that they'd pay it no heed.

But they remained true to their mute God. Never rising to meet me. In fact, the only retort my father made in ten years of gibing and needling comprised of a single word: 'Faith. F-A-I-T-H!' he spelled out, as if that would elucidate the wispy vagueness of his spirituality. 'A simple matter of belief, son. It supersedes science, and logic, and rationality.'

My father believed, evidently, in his calm condescension, that he'd made his point and that it was definitive. It was the only moment where I felt so much as even grudging respect for him, while my mother smiled affectionately at me and offered a faintly pious, and what I still to this day consider to be a palpably sinister, 'Thank you.' As if to say, 'Thank you, Albert. I'm glad you've come around. We're delighted you're with us now.'

Thank you, I thought. *Fuck you!* was more like it. But I ran out of rage shortly after and just walked away from them.

My siblings, an older sister and two younger brothers, are a different matter entirely. I have always experienced them as distant abstractions, not quite people at all. I repeatedly fail to feel close to them, simply because it is impossible for me to contrive love where there isn't even familiarity.

The way they willed the warped values of our parents upon themselves, and bathed in uncritical conformity, left me utterly disaffected. They just morphed with evolutionary slowness into watery versions of the two idiots without raising so much as a single enlightened question in their entire existence. Automatons, this is what my siblings are and what I fear most in myself; death by dumb compliance.

'They're too dull to be alive,' I often complained to Val. I'd always felt it so. Instinctively. So I committed to trailblazing a better path for myself; a path more true, and refined, and anthropologically evolved. 'I have no time for family,' I would tell her, 'because everything I know of it further demonstrates the futility and stupidity of all human life.'

To which Val would respond, 'Thank you, Al,' and then go on about her radio programmes and residents' meetings and gossip and disappointment over my retarded ambition.

She knew I didn't mean her. She knows me. And she knows

I'm not wrong either...

So anyway, I sat for dinner. Yes...

Under emotional duress. She still holds that unusual sway over me. The ability to make me feel bad rather than afraid. I suppose that in itself is proof, was it needed, that I do still love her; the innate reluctance to displease...

Love is not the issue, no. Absolutely not. But passion is. And frustration. They're all in the mix. I have held these emotions, and sometimes the lack of them, against her without comprehending, quite, the wricked and pernicious nature of my resentment...

Having grown weary and irritated by my middle-age, my frustration with my lot has come to be expressed through dissatisfaction with my wife. Precisely how the disdain I had for the innumerable ills amassed by society was bound up in the vivacious and strident personage of Val, is hard to fathom. Even for me. Val, after all, sharply mischievous and ardently purposeful in all her endeavours and relations, is in many respects the antithesis of modern life; a bland, listless, homogenous, impersonal, lazy, and trite affair. But she has. Somehow she has become the focal point for my immense dissatisfaction. My sense of having failed at life.

Her enthusiastic embracing of change, her perpetual rising to the new; it feels like a deplorable betrayal. As if the whole thing—our marriage—was a game that she never bothered to fully explain. A game that I've spent a lifetime trying to impose earnest sense upon only to discover there are no rules and she knew it all along...

'It's just to be lived!' she said once, as if that was something everybody knew...

I was fucking shocked to hear it, if you must know. Left out of the loop, as I've said. The only fucking moron at the party! Sometimes I feel as if that is what I've been. All my life...

And this thought occurred to me just then, as I looked at her across the kitchen table: *You've known all along and never bloody told me!*

'So, I met Nicky Jones,' she said, her eyebrow singing and soaring like a swallow.

'So you said.'

'He's dating somebody on staff. Apparently.'

'He's what?'

'Yeah, I thought that would get your attention,' she grinned. 'You've barely touched your dinner,' she added in a quick and shrewish aside, nodding at my plate. 'But, yes, dating. In-house. Not wise, I don't think. And I told him as much.'

'Who? Who's he with?'

'I don't know. He wouldn't say.'

'So why tell you at all then?'

'Well exactly. That's what I wondered.'

'Impossible.' I shook my head.

'I think you're wrong on this one, Al. Taking advantage of one of those naïve and nubile young ones, I bet. But, I mean, he's seriously overweight, Al.'

You think I can't see that? He's repellent. 'What do you want me to do about it?'

'Nothing. I'm just telling you.'

'No you're not. The tone you used, it was accusatory. As if I'm somehow responsible for him.' *For his lardy abominableness,* I said, looking down at my own stomach and the doughy seal of blubber disgorging over my belt-line. 'How many times do I have to point this out, Val—I am not the school. I exist, as a distinct individual, beyond its parameters. I don't care what the people I work with do in their spare time.'

'That's ridiculous, Al. First of all, you cannot spend twenty-five years in a place and not be part of the fabric, no matter what you say. But I was simply making the point that your fat line-manager, and professional senior, seems to have bagged a girl against all odds. That's all.'

'No you weren't, Val. You weren't just saying. You were accusing. First and foremost. And, what's more, you're instigating a rumour. Sidling up cosy with idle gossip, for the pure malicious fun of it.'

'Oh come off the high horse, Al. And your head fairly shot up when I told you, I might add. Don't even bother denying it.'

'I was momentarily curious, sure. But for a moment only, and by the implausibility of it as much as anything. As any lewd act might draw attention. But we're supposed to be civilised, Val. And civilisation is as much a matter of resisting our basest indulgences, and refining our interests, as it is a celebration of the crude facts of what we are. I'm sure we could all be out killing and fornicating. But we choose otherwise, don't we?'

'Sure, Al. Sure. Why not, but indulge me here. Put your good taste aside and speculate for me. Who could it be?' Val lifted a pencil and began writing on the back of the receipt from the hardware store that lay on the table beside my weapons, pushed aside for dinner. She looked at them for the first time, wondering, surely, how she had sat down and not tidied them away. 'What's all this about anyway? Rope? What do you need rope for?' she asked.

I almost laughed. For the irony of it. But resisted. 'Hanging stuff. In the garden, I've…' I didn't quite know myself what purpose I had in mind for the rope. For any of it. I just felt that there was enough there to do the job.

Val shook her head, writing off my bumbling secretiveness. 'Right, let's make a list. The unmarried, first. Then we'll subdivide them into age profiles. I bet we can figure this out in half an hour. Let's out the bitch!'

The conclusion that Val reached, no matter how much I resisted it, was unthinkable. Having ruled out the marrieds, the list was reduced to the seventeen remaining members of staff. The possibility of a male lover was mooted—'In the interests of thoroughness, Val, it must be considered. We can't just dismiss possibilities because they don't quite agree with some presupposed outcome.' But Val made short work of Nicholas Jones's homosexuality with some spurious though popular generalizations—'For firstly, he's too fat,' she said. Gay men weren't fat, apparently. None of them. And he had no observable dress-sense or subtlety of manner. Not to mention that he was happy, and it was a well-known, even if somewhat of a political hot potato, that gays, all of them, were fundamentally unhappy people; oddly incomplete, and tragic. Whereas Nicholas Jones was, *'Almost emphatic in his mediocrity.'* Utterly lacking in tragedy, *'A man of laughable inconsequence.'* Until now.

My heart broke for the obscenity of Val's simple convictions. Conservative and prejudicial, they had sneaked upon her at the turn of forty and placed a figurative flag in the ideological ground, claiming her as the continuation of a genealogical line; a racial heritage of bigotry, classism, elitism, and conservatism, insidiously espoused through a myriad of subtle disapprovals and knowing whispers. She had become her parents' daughter, just as they had been begotten of theirs, and so on, all the way back through the ages; cultural memories of superiority asserting themselves. I might have walked out on the marriage there and then for the offensiveness of her opinions alone had they not simultaneously prompted laughter. In my pouffed guffaw there was a reminder of some untellable essence of her, of some once known delightfulness that I had lost touch with. A brief nostalgia, for her openness, her naivety, her surety in the permanence of things, all things, lifted the oppression of discontent that was hovering above the table in our family kitchen.

'It's Aimeé Quinn then,' she declared, emphatically. 'Who else? There's nobody else, is there?'

Having seen the inevitable conclusion slightly in advance of its arrival, I wept. Silently. As the numbers dwindled, as colleagues were struck from Val's list, systematically and with a degree of sound deduction, I could see who was slowly being unveiled as Jones's most unlikely, yet plausible, bride.

'It can't be.' I stared at the plate of food Val had insisted upon placing before me. 'Afraid not, Val. There must be some mistake.'

'He told me himself, Al. A member of staff. Younger—he said that!'

'Unmarried? Female? Did he say any of that?'

'Come on, Al, he's not gay. We both know that. And unmarried, well, okay, so I'm assuming that. But even taking that away and narrowing it down to the younger, which we know, and the female, which we are more or less certain about, how many does that leave? Four or five? Three of which are married. There are really only two possibilities—Jane Hempenstall and Aimeé Quinn. It has to be Aimeé!'

'Why?' I blurted out. 'Why does it have to be Aimeé Quinn? I don't accept that at all. What's wrong with Hempenstall?'

'The fact that you refer to her as Hempenstall is a fair indication. As if she's just another one of the boys from the locker room. Men don't come across all boastful about women like Jane Hempenstall, Al. I'm telling you, Nicky Jones is positively delighted with himself.'

'And what about all the other assumptions you're making? All the others you're ruling out? It's not very scientific, is it? I mean even the fact that you're taking Jones's story at face value, without corroboration…'

'He's not going to tell a lie like that, Al. Whatever he is, it isn't stupid. There's too much room for embarrassment. I think we can be fairly confident the story he's telling is true.'

'Jones is not fucking Aimeé Quinn, Val! That is self-evident, surely!'

'It certainly is not, Albert. Some women like a big man. And he's her superior, technically speaking. There's always something in that. It facilitates a man punching above his weight.'

'An unfortunate expression,' I grumbled.

'But none the less, that's what he's doing.'

'No. He isn't. I just know, Val. You're wrong on this. It can't be.'

'Why not? A little thing for the Quinn girl, have we, Al?'

'Don't be ridiculous. But I've seen her. With other colleagues, and how awkward they all are around him. With his gormless blather.'

'You say gormless, Al, but he's actually quite engaging. Gregarious. Once you get talking with him. I can see a certain charm to him, for a younger woman, especially.'

I rose from the table. 'I'm taking the dog for a walk,' I said. 'Enough of the Chinese whispers! Enough gossip. I'm not quite sure how you drew me into this, but I'm done with it now.' *Leave the fat bastard to himself. And her, if she's that fucking stupid,* I added.

'We really have touched a nerve here, haven't we, Al?' she teased. 'Are we suddenly feeling the creeping hand of middle-age? Has your spindly ego been piqued? No longer the most handsome man on staff?'

'No, Val. It hasn't. I'm as self-contained as I've ever been.' I slipped my feet into my unlaced trainers, picked up the dog's leash and ushered him toward the front door. 'Oh, one of the children called, by the way,' I said. 'The boy. You can call him and discuss it, if you like.' *He'd be a more receptive ear to this kind of puerile bullshit…*

The dog trotted onwards, coursing through the estate, leading me open-eyed but far away. We crossed the road, through onto the spongy turf track down to the shore, the dog's nose a trusty beacon.

How could she? I thought. Aimeé and Jones? *My Aimeé.*

Val's got to be wrong, I assured myself before conceding the credibleness of it. But even if it were true, and I could barely hold myself together at the thought, then it could only be the most recent of developments, and was, therefore, susceptible to derailment. Embryonic unions are the most vulnerable to outside forces, after all. Easy prey to all sorts of insubstantial maliciousness. The Quinn-Jones union, were it truly true, could be severed.

The impetus for action came to me lyrically, spoken in a voice shorn of its comic affectation: 'People who are uglier than you or I…' sang in my mind. Pop wisdom from my young adulthood, reaching further than its meaning. Take what you need. And leave. A fragment. Wit without context; it passed for revelation and brought a sigh—'Indeed, *A Rush and a Push and the Land is Ours.*'

It's as simple as that, I thought, as I passed a gaggle of giggling girls on their way back up from the beach, some of whom no doubt I would have known had I been aware enough to look up from the dog's shimmering tail, weaving a path for me to absently follow. *Take what you need!* This is the very mantra!

After all, politeness and patience—how had they served me? The connotations, I knew instantly, were violent. This was free-market speak, capitalist ideology extended to the sphere of intimate relations. Appealing to the strong and putting fear in the weak. For years I had performed as a weak man would—trying to be fair, and considerate and reasonable and unassuming. But the newfound clarity of purpose, knowing precisely what it was—who it was—that I now desired—and who I didn't, for that matter—empowered me. There were no more moral conundrums to neutralise my base desires, no sense of obligation or fear of disapproval to cow me. The desired outcome had crystalised, and now the method to be invoked was known. It all but chose itself, really. If unhappiness equalled X, and happiness equalled Y, and X and Y could never coexist, well then I needed to cancel X and appropriate Y.

I had no doubt that X could be easily cancelled but I was greatly concerned with the unverifiable velocity with which Y was reported to have been receding from me. Aimeé Quinn, Little Miss Y, could very well be out of reach entirely if I didn't act forthwith.

But Aimeé is not lost, it naturally followed. *She is not lost, not lost yet, not lost to me yet!* I said, paving the way for premeditation.

The sun had dipped and with it the searing burn of the day. I drifted to less brainsickly thoughts in the fresh air, in the open spaces of the coastline. The clammy evening flushed across me, caressing my torso beneath the loosely hung polo shirt, and the trousers of my light summer suit felt just about custom-made for the weather. In my beige, flat-soled trainers I was pitifully incoherent. Head to toe.

I walked on, led by the dog's unremitting desire to be submerged by the sea, to lap it up and luxuriate in it, contemplating how out of touch I was; had always been. Ill-fitted to my time, I sometimes felt. Like those mad old men of my youth who spent hours fishing for nothing off the harbour; wearing singlets with rings of yellowed sweat under the arms. Or sat drinking coffees or spirits on the pavement tables in town; hour after hour, day after day, wearing clothes from decades past. Or sometimes they could be seen wearing a bright cap or some unusually trendy footwear, a present from a son or daughter, or grandchild, but worn without consideration for taste or style. How strange they had been to me, and how I had wondered of them then—*How did you end up like this? So removed from objective opinion? From conformity?*

You must know you look ridiculous, I thought to myself, as a boy, looking upon these old men.

But now I had become one of them; casually dismissive of the perplexity I incited in the young. I didn't care what teenage girls would make of my apparently random attire. My world was no longer concerned with such triviality. I was a man whose solace lay in the fundamental elements of human life—time, the distinct ruminations of my own mind, philosophies of life and love.

Long forgotten by the world, those men seem wise to me now, and thoughts of them stir up a reticent respect. A reverence that stops me, momentarily, as I consider the forces that could have driven those poor souls from their homes.

What regrets drive men into wide open solitude?

Their wives, their children? Their own relentless thoughts?

I felt I knew exactly, out there as I was, walking the dog, in flight from my wife and, indeed, my very life.

I was just like those men, in fact. So content in my aloneness that I could gladly have walked the length and breadth of the strand wearing nothing at all. Just to be alive for half an hour. Away from that house, that existence, where the habits of a lifetime had beaten me down ...

The dog scuttled between the bollards that marked the beginning of the coastal walkway, onto a tarmacked path over the sparsely vegetated dunes that ran the length of the beach, and I followed after. I prefer to walk the path, to stay away from the uneven pebbles and the shifting gradient of the narrow beach, but the dog hauled me ever onwards, toward the sea, and in doleful mood I submitted to the poor mongrel's simple will.

At the waterside I took off my trainers and socks and rolled up my trousers, letting the dog off the leash. I sat down, grinding my toes between the loose pebbles and into the sand, and watched the dog collide kamikaze-like with the crushing waves, only to emerge yelping and thrilled, barking, his thick coat soaked, and ready to bound in and go again. Intermittently he returned to me, tongue hanging loose with exhaustion, seeking an affirmative patting or a 'Good boy.' And he'd sit down beside me, looking out to sea, wondering, perhaps, just what the wonder was, before cascading down to the water again.

That, I thought, looking down, *is about the size of her head.*

I had been scraping into the sand using a stone, in a roughly circular and downward motion, without realizing. My fingernails were packed full of damp sand and I had dug a hole deep enough to lay Val's head in.

This is where I'll bury her, I thought, thinking of it for the first time as a form of reality. I looked out along the sheened surface of the sea, toward the horizon, and drank in the promise of freedom. Inebriating myself with idealised nothings. With hazy dreams of new beginnings.

I wondered would I miss her and felt I wouldn't. *I love her,* I said over and over in my mind, addressing an imagined jury of my peers. *And while I still love her for all the beauty that has passed between us, the essence of our affection is now in the past.* It had, in fact, passed. That fact was irrefutable. I needed to move on, to make use of the time afforded me by the fluke of life. There was no time to waste. *Something has to give,* I explained in my imagined defence, and though it saddened me, she was it. *I'll bury her in sand, at night, in a grave dug with my hands at low tide, and let the sea wash her to eternity,* I spoke quietly, studying my sanded fingers and palms ...

'Al! Hey, Al,' somebody said. 'Crackin' evening down here, isn't it?'

I looked around.

Jane Hempenstall; her beefy white legs, surprisingly smooth and clean of hair, hanging like some dry-cured Spanish hams from her khaki shorts, pounding towards me. Looking quickly upward from the spectacle of her lower body, I saw what I was long acclimatised to—her in her hockey club, mustard T-shirt. It was beat onto her. Ridges of flesh over-spilling, and her fat, squashed breasts spread thickly across her chest.

I dusted the sand from my hands and stood up. 'Yeah, it's beautiful alright.'

'How're you keeping?'

'Good, Jane. All good, thanks. How're the dogs?' I asked, glancing at the surly pit-bull and the deceptively placid boxer that stood obediently either side of her.

She smiled proudly. 'Oh, great. You know yourself, Al, they just love it down here. Dog's life and all that.'

'Yeah,' I replied, somewhat confused by her errant employment of idiom. Then I blurted out, involuntarily. 'Have you heard about Jones?'

'What do you mean?'

'That he's been ... well, you know ... with another member of staff?'

'He what?' she shrieked.

'Yeah, you know, like ... dating. Or something.'

'Jeeze! Really? No, I hadn't actually. Heard nothing. Who do you think it could be?' she asked.

'Well, we could narrow it down quickly enough, I suppose.'

'I wouldn't know where to begin. Honestly.'

'I mean how many single women are there on staff? That's where you'd start, isn't it?'

'Assuming it's one of the singles. And that it's not a man, of course. I find him a little camp,' Jane added.

My heart fluttered to life. 'Oh, right. Do you think that's a possibility?'

'Eh ... no. Suppose not,' she said, dashing my hopes. 'When you think about it. Man or woman, it hardly matters. I mean, and I know it's pots and kettles, but just look at him.'

'You're nothing like that, Jane.' *He's a slob and* 'You're ...'

Jane Hempenstall isn't one of the multitudes for whom I hold only contempt. She is, in fact, eminently tolerable. The only fat person I know that I actually like ...

'I'm widely spread. Big joints and limbs, Al. Don't embarrass yourself. I know what I am. But there's nothing more I can do. And, you know, I diet. I do. And I exercise—you see me out here ... but there's just a point I can't get beyond.'

'Sorry,' I said. *I would never even want to put you and him in the same sentence, Jane. Honestly.*

'Forget it,' she said. 'Well, the only ones I know who are single are me and—now—Aimeé. Since a few weeks ago, I hear. And it isn't me, I can assure you. So?'

'So you think it could be Aimeé?'

'Not really,' Jane said, suddenly, on reflection.

A flush of relief ran through me.

'But, on the other hand, brokenhearted girls will do the dumbest things. Maybe it's a rash kind of rebound or something. Maybe,' she added...

The last light was fading as I rounded the gateway, the dog now in tow to me. I let it through the side gate and locked it.

At the front door I kicked off my trainers and shook the sand out of my socks, before opening the door and stepping inside in bare feet. I felt the wet ends of my trousers draping over my ankles as I stood in the hallway listening for Val's whereabouts. Seeing the light cast by the TV over the darkened landing, through the open door of the master bedroom, I knew she would be soon asleep.

I unbuckled my trousers, stepped out of them, and walked to the kitchen, where I jotted down a merged itinerary and inventory onto blank piece of paper: *rope; saw; after midnight; tarpaulin from shed; shovel (just in case); phone children in the morning; clean the car?; carwash out of town; back before dawn; go to work; seek out Aimeé; breakfast; police?...*

Witness Interview 4.
Jane Hempenstall, 42, Teacher

AL AND ME GOT ALONG just fine, as it happens. I wouldn't say we were friends, but we got along. I really liked him.

It was a beautiful evening down there, I remember that. Really peaceful. That view—wow! It's just stunning on an evening like that. It brings people to the shore. Walking dogs, holding hands, passing time. And Al was with his dog. Normal as anything if you looked about you. Just like the rest of us. He was just sitting there on the sand, watching the dog in the water. Lost in his thoughts. Didn't even notice me till I was right on top of him and called his name. I just figured he was enjoying the view. A bit of time to himself.

What did we speak about? Nothing much. I asked how Val was? He asked how the dogs were. Small talk. A bit of gossip about school. And I suppose that was unusual because I don't think I ever remember Al gossiping. But I suppose I just thought that he felt freer out there on the beach, away from the school, with just me and him. Maybe he felt he could loosen up a bit. Because we got on well, like I said. He was such a gentleman, you see. I know, it must be hard for people to hear that, but he really was.

I'm not sure if I should really be talking about it. The gossip. I mean, I already told the police. But that was official, wasn't it? And no offence, Mr. Vaughan, but you're not the law, are you?

A reporter?

Oh, a novelist. Right, well okay. But still, gossiping between two colleagues is one thing, but telling a man carrying a dictaphone is another, if you get my meaning.

All I can say is that Al was—and I hesitate to say this—unusually interested in the private life of one of our colleagues. I'll name no names but what Al suspected was that a certain member of staff was involved with a certain other member of staff. We were gossiping, basically, wondering who it could be. Anyway, we reached a conclusion, quickly enough, after ruling me out. Which we both laughed at. But I wouldn't like to say who. It wouldn't be fair. What I will say is that I wondered, after hearing what happened to Val ... Look, I don't know anything for sure. You never know what goes on inside people's hearts, do you? Like I said, I've no proof of anything.

I know the knee-jerk mob probably want to get hold of Al right now and string him up, but I'm a big fat liberal on these things. I can only imagine that for a man like Al to commit a thing like that there must have been some awful pain going on inside him. I'd suggest—knowing nothing, of course—that he must have just broke down in some way. And if there's anything I could do to help fix him, I'd be happy to do it. I don't care what people say, you know. But I'd understand too if Al never wants to be fixed. To have to face that, with a straight head on his shoulders? It might not be worth it.

Five

... WHETHER I WAS HUNGRY or procrastinating is a moot point: I made myself tea and toast and sat down at the kitchen table.

The room was lit only by a dim strip light above the counter. I buttered the toast heavily so that it pooled in pockets of oily yellow on the crumby surface, before soaking in and leaving the bread warm and soggy, just as I like it. With the middle and index fingers of my left hand looped in the handle of the mug, elbow on the table, slightly slouched over, I picked up the triangular cut toast in my right, and moved it to my mouth. As I did so, I became preoccupied by the peculiar fluidity and steadiness of the movement. I raised my hand to eye-level and examined it—dead still. *A surgeon's hand. A gunslinger's. Some Yul Brynner type, enshadowed and driven by mystery, or a higher calling; some inherent virtuousness not fully understood even by himself.*

My tea was beginning to grey and all that remained of the toast were the fallen granules on the floral tablecloth. I placed the mug on the empty plate and pushed them both aside, stretching out across the table to pull the pruning saw and the rope over. I held the pruning saw out in front of me, resting it in my open palms, and considered its weight. Its clinical morbidity. I withdrew it from the plastic sheath. *It's scabbard!* I said, and studied the razor teeth and the feel of the D-handle; the laminated wood felt slippy in my palm and I wondered would I need gloves too.

From my pocket I then took my phone, zipping through a line of photos until I came to the one I was looking for. Taken nearly four months previously, at the end of year drinks. A handful of colleagues, glasses raised, late on into the evening, posing for posterity; a meaningless moment, had it not been for the presence of Aimeé Quinn, slightly wide of centre in the back row. *How everything seems to attach itself to you,* I whispered. How everyone found themselves evaluated in light of how they matched up to her. Wherever she went. Whatever the context.

There was a perfect radiance to her. Something purely innocent, even angelic, and yet somehow sultry. When I looked at that photo all I could really think of is what her bare breasts might look like, in the half light, plump above me, her hair swept back with one hand, pivoting and rocking in ecstasy across my hips. I even dared to finger the screen gently, touching the curve of her barely suggested breast in the summer green dress she'd worn that night.

I ache for your gentle face.

I gazed at it, anxious then to begin the process of bringing her home to me.

I took the shovel and the saw and placed them carefully in the boot of Val's car. At the foot of the stairs I picked up the rope, tarpaulin and a mallet; the mallet a last minute addition, found resting by the door of the shed when I'd gone to fetch the tarpaulin. In contortions of exaggerated silence, I joined the dots up the stairs, carefully attempting to avoid each known creak but, even in bare feet, failing to do so. Travelling as lightly up the stairs as possible, there was a single elusive moment where the miserable ineptitude of my agenda struck me and caused me to stand frozen on the stairs, one knee bent to my abdomen as my foot stretched to two steps above. But the desperate fear, the dread, of Aimeé slipping away hurled me back into motion; moving tragically forward, crazed and terrified by the rising waters of my most imminent fantasies.

There was momentum in my feet, and my hands, but everything else lagged behind; emotions, uncontrollable and desperate, swirling and dizzying. Time was out of sync. It appropriated my thoughts exactly as they were, in their entirety—unfiltered, uncensored, untested. Propelling me forward, faster than I could reason, ignorant of the past, incapable of seeing the future. Circumstances dictated my actions, ensnaring me in some princely obligation of state. I imagined myself the reluctant protagonist, the man with fortitude and wit enough to match the sinister forces in cahoots against him. I was a crusader, a pioneer, a maverick riding at destiny's shoulder.

Exhilaration, of the type that can only be felt in a moment of pure immorality, surged, and for a moment, imagining a scene where the lights would suddenly come on and expose me— halfway up the stairs, armed to the teeth for brutality, somehow Neanderthal in my hairy feet and fish-eyed intent—I rushed to conclusion.

The landing was crossed swiftly, the bedroom carefully.

In the flicker of the TV light, I stood over the bed. Her body heaved under the duvet, wrapped tight around her turned shoulder. My eyes watered a little as I tightened the grip on the mallet's handle. There was a moment where I wanted to walk away, when I just might have, but then she stirred.

My arm flexed. Explosively. Knuckles to shoulder—a dull and ineffective thump!

In the glare of my own atrocity, I was paralytic, watching as her expression recovered from shock unbounded. But when she yelled out, in pain and horror, and her eyes caught mine one final time, I brought an end to her. With the swiftest and shallowest of backswings. A surprisingly crisp crack across the temporal plate...

Part II

Simon Atley

'I WAS OFF MY TITS on some highly suspect ganja, right,' he
admitted, straight off. 'But I know what I saw. It came in the
post the day before, see. A mate of mine. Not technically illegal.
Not on any banned substances list. Some mutant fucking plant
from the Republic of Marley, you know what I'm saying. But
my mate, who shall remain nameless, okay, he ...'

'Simon,' I interjected, in a way that had been typical of the interview to that point. It had taken near enough two hours just to get
Atley's recollections from earlier on in the day onto tape in any kind of
comprehensible form. 'You're losing your way again. Can you focus on
what you saw exactly? What was said between you and Mr. Jackson?
Did he engage with you? Or you with him? How did it start?'

Atley had been trundling home, stoned to his eyeballs. He had
cut in through a housing estate on the outskirts of town, intend-
ing to somehow mount the six-foot perimeter wall to the rear
of it and cross the wasteland towards his own home. Away from
the main road and in the quiet of the estate, he spotted what he
described as 'the grass of the gods,' among the many manicured
lawns. He stumbled heavy-footed through a flower bed, crushing
and unearthing the late-blooming red roses of autumn and gladi-
olus stems, before lowering himself onto the grass and rolling onto
his back. Arms and legs outstretched, he drifted dopily, encased in
the midnight air, lost to the stars and foggy-headedness.

An indeterminate length of time passed before he became
aware of the straining, the laboured breath, and a plastic rustle
from the driveway. He watched quietly as the man attempted to
haul and leverage a package into the open boot of a car.

He described the scene as like watching 'a man with a fucking huge fish,' the way it kept slipping out and away from his

grasp. Then, upon suddenly recognising the man and forgetting himself, he called out, 'Alright, Sir? Need a hand?'

He tripped onto his feet and over towards the car. He recalled that Mr. Jackson made one final attempt to quickly manoeuvre the package into the boot, and almost achieved it, before he arrived and took hold of the other end and helped hoist it in.

'Sir stood there, just staring at me. Freaked the shit out of me. I must have just known something, you know. And he knew I knew. The way he looked. I could feel it. Right in my bones. I got a sick sense for that kind of thing. Seen the killer in his eyes. Creeped me out. I should be on CSI or something. The real CSI. No joke! I just got something. A gift. Something extraterrestrial, you know. And when I looked down—her fucking foot! No shit! Sticking out the end of the bag. He slammed the boot closed pretty quick. But he knew! I saw it. No doubt.'

Mr. Jackson thanked him, Atley claimed. 'Cold. Like proper fucking ice, you know. In his veins. Thanked me! Fuck me! Never seen anything like it.'

Mr. Jackson proceeded to ask Atley a couple of questions, the precise details of which were beyond Atley's powers of recall. 'I'd got nothing to say at that point anyway,' he pointed out.

The next thing Atley remembered was jumping backwards to avoid the reversing car as he stood immobilised at the end of driveway, rooted by mortal fear. 'I was that close, when you think about it,' he said. 'Could have been me next. No doubt about it. Easy as.'

'What did you do then?' I asked.

'What did I do? A moment of fucking clarity, that's what I done. Out with the phone. Rang the cops—not something I'm too likely for doing, to be fair. They had no interest though. Didn't want to know about it. Not at first. 'Specially when I told them he was my teacher. But I wouldn't let it go. I told them, 'Come and get me. I'm going nowhere. Can't fucking walk anyway.' The rotten ganja or the post-traumatic, I couldn't say. But I told them, straight-up, 'Look, I'm proper fucking melted here, but I know what I seen. And I'll fucking testify,' I told them. Swore to them. 'I can't be silenced.' I said that to them. Straight-up.'

So Simon Atley rang the police, swearing blind that he'd

seen a human foot dangling from the bound package he had helped his English teacher load into a car boot in the middle of the night. The police, naturally, were sceptical, given the boy's record; a mosaic of infraction and misdemeanour.

When the police arrived it was discretely, with steps so prudent as to be apathetic; a lone car gliding quietly through the estate, siren muted and emergency roof-light sloping woozily around with all the urgency of a maudlin drunk. The attending officers began not with the crime but the self-styled whistle-blower. In agitated whispers at the bottom of the driveway, the first thing they wanted to know was why Atley was there at all. And only then why he had been helping Mr. Jackson, and what precisely it was he was claiming to have seen. After hearing Atley out, and observing him, they insisted on knowing how much he had smoked or ingested, and of what, before they would even consider ringing the bell on the Jackson family home at twenty minutes after one a.m.

By the time they deemed the strength of Atley's conviction to outweigh his dubious credentials, he had been threatened with an admirable array of charges, the real and custom-made: trespass, wilful waste of police resources, possession of imported narcotics, public disorder, malicious deceit, libel, theft, and loitering with mal-intent.

But on their approach to the Jacksons' house they found the front door wide open and a broken window. Their attention was then drawn to some questionable markings on the driveway. When nobody came to the door, the bell having been rung, they felt they had sufficient cause to enter the premises. Upon entry, they discovered a bloodied garment hanging partially out of the kitchen bin, on foot of which they decided to wake Officers Anthony Tallis and Denise Howard from their night's sleep, enquiring about the scene they had attended at the Jackson household late the previous afternoon. On the basis of their input the attending officers began knocking on some neighbours' doors, finally putting out an alert for any sightings of a green Estate car or any suspicious activity in the general coastal area.

Simon Atley was driven home around three a.m. and left in the care of his parents.

Jay Holmes: attending officer at the Jackson household

JAY HOLMES WAS THE MOST senior Officer at the Jackson household that night. He had no dealings with Mr Jackson in person, although it was he who ultimately triggered the alert. He arrived at the Jackson household at 01:10 (approx). Of Simon Atley, Officer Holmes said: 'He was well-known to us, without being considered a threat. Too stupid to be a threat, really.'

When I put it to him that Simon Atley was instrumental in the apprehension of Mr. Jackson, Officer Holmes was eager to play down Atley's significance. 'He alerted us, sure, but we could not have proceeded on his word alone. It was the circumstantial stuff that tipped the decision. The broken window. Nobody home. Markings on the driveway. The front door wide open. A bloodied shirt, for Jesus sake! You didn't have to be Columbo! A TV light upstairs was visible from the porch. The dog in the back was going barking mad. The kid tipped us off, but that wouldn't have meant anything had the scene itself not matched up. And we found small traces of blood upstairs too. On the bed and carpet. Hers. Murderers are rarely clever. If they were, they wouldn't murder. It's a messy crime, and statistically they don't evade capture. That scumbag was caught on the strength of police expertise. He may have conned himself a bed in the psych. house, but he's not out there walking the streets, at least. And that's thanks to police professionalism, not some stonehead.'

When I asked Officer Holmes on what basis he believed that Mr. Jackson had *conned* himself into the Reil Institute, he admitted he had no facts. 'The same way I knew the crime scene was a crime scene, that's how,' he said. 'Because I've seen it all before.'

In the end, Officer Holmes became greatly irritated by my questions and ended the interview. He told me to read the papers. Told me it was all there in black and white.

John Baros and Ross O'Connell: the arresting officers at the beach

OF THE ARRESTING OFFICERS - Officer John Baros and Officer Ross O'Connell - only O'Connell was prepared to talk with me in person. Officer Baros, citing what seemed a plausible unwillingness to speculate beyond anything factual, eventually agreed to provide me with his written statement, which he sent to me via the care of Professor Novak.

Arresting officer 1 : John Baros

Unofficial Statement on the arrest of Mr Albert Jackson on the 28th September at 05:30 (approx.), by Officer John Baros

On approach to the Bayside layby a single car was evident. The layby is an unofficial carpark that locals use to access the beach. The car was a green Estate car. It matched a description received on general alert earlier in our shift.

On inspection the car had no significant markings or damage to the exterior. The doors were unlocked but closed. The engine was cold.

The morning was calm but cool. It was approaching high tide. A lone individual was observed sitting down close to the water's edge. There then turned out to be two individuals. The one sitting down was a male. His name was Albert Jackson. Aged 49. Local teacher. The second individual was Valerie Jackson. She was Mr. Jackson's spouse. She was found to be deceased.

Sticking out of the sand was a heavy-duty gardening spade. A length of rope lay beside it. A tarpaulin sheet was later found blowing in the dunes. It was matched to the crime scene.

Mr. Jackson did not respond to any questions. He looked out to sea. He did not move. Both his arms had a hold of the victim. They ran under her arms. His hands joined across her chest.

The victim was buried to her waist in the sand. The torso of the victim lay back against Mr. Jackson's upper thighs and stomach. Her head hung to the right. The sea was washing up to her waist. Mr. Jackson was wet to his waist when escorted from the beach. He didn't speak.

Arresting officer 2: Ross O'Connell

Officer O'Connell was affable and relaxed, though clearly troubled by the events of the night in question. He didn't know the Jacksons personally, he said, being from out of town, but a lot of people in his social circle knew them. 'Particularly Mr. Jackson,' he said.

Of Officer O'Connell's friends who knew Mr. Jackson, they all seemed to have known him as a teacher. Anecdotally, Mr. Jackson seemed to have positioned himself somewhere between a stuffy but likeable pedant and an entirely inconsequential oddity. I was unsure, at first, why Officer O'Connell might have been so affected by what he saw. But over the course of the conversation I came to both trust and sympathise with what he told me. He was genuinely unsettled by what happened Mrs. Jackson, and by how Mr. Jackson presented upon arrest.

'I'd never seen a dead body before. Not like that anyway. You know what I mean? A murdered dead body. Seen some in funeral parlours but this was different.'

O'Connell's elucidation on how it was different proved rambling, but demonstrated a peculiar empathy for both the victim and the offender:

The whole scene was wrong. She was cold. Freezing in that water. Her hair. And her eyes—oh my fuck, her eyes! They were open. But dead, you know. It's all in the eyes. Our whole life. And when it's gone, you can see it. But there was him too, and the morning. It was beautiful. Clear blue skies just starting to brighten up. The water calm. It was so quiet though. And he was quiet. Calm. Didn't flinch as we approached. And we were calling out to him. No doubt he heard us. He didn't want to cover anything up. I'm sure of that. He was just waiting to get picked up. So fucking still though—frightening. Horrible. And that's what's fucked me up more than anything about all this, you know. How sad he was.

On psych leave now, so I am. Still. Been talking and talking it through with this woman from outside town. All paid for, you know.

Her eyes was the thing, at first. Open. I wasn't ready to see that. But then other stuff, stuff I didn't think I even noticed, started coming at me in the night. Her hair, all matted. Heavy, like rope or something. And her soaked clothes. She looked... abandoned. She was like some fucked-up old building, or some haggard street kid or something. There was something gone from inside her. Everything grey. Greys and blues. Pale and dark blues. That's what the whole morning was made of. That's what I can't shake—the atmosphere that hung there. Over all of us. And even him—and this is what I'm saying—as the time passed this is what played on me as much as her. That stare out to sea. Into nothing at all. Agony. Real pain—the kind that just shuts you up so tight you can't move. And him holding her. Holding her! She's half fucking buried and he's holding her! His face just ruined, you know.

'Face of a killer,' I heard one guy say back at the station. 'Never forget it once you've seen it.' And I nodded away at the time. I've no problem telling anyone that. But it wasn't what I thought. But I didn't know what to say. Didn't know what I'd seen, really. What I thought. But since then I've just been getting the feeling that that wasn't what I saw. It just wasn't the face of a killer, you know. That's the thing that's messing me up. That Mr. Jackson looked shook, to be honest. Right down to his boots. Rocked all the way through. Never looked like crying, mind. I'm not saying that. But the way he moved with us. The total stillness of the man. The staring. No responses to anything. And then I heard about his statement. Like the way he made a little story out of the whole thing, and I just thought, What a sick bastard! You know?

But I couldn't sleep for that look on his face. I couldn't get it to fit with the story that was coming out. With the facts. I made myself sick feeling some kind of sympathy for the guy. In the end I just had to sign off work. Had to talk to somebody.

It's the look on his face, you know.

Eyes? The whole face? Something he said or did? I don't know. He sure didn't say anything, so we can rule that out. But how we found him, that isn't what the papers say. Or the guys at the station. That's all I'm saying.

Maybe he was fucking mad for a minute, sane for a minute, mad for a minute, sane for a minute ... you know. Or maybe he got half an hour of his right mind down there on the beach and it just happens that that was when we picked him up.

I don't know. That's all I'm saying, I guess. I don't know.

Novak and me

PROFESSOR NOVAK AGREED to meet me in Terri Carlson's to discuss how we should proceed. I made sure I arrived fifteen minutes early, with the intention of being in my seat and braced for his arrival. Arriving early and prepared was to be my tardy retaliation to the imbalance created by our first encounter. I hoped that by displacing him from his natural environ, the Reil—the seat of his esteem—I could unsettle him.

I had my collated facts and testimonies, queries and conundrums, assembled and ready to hurl at him. From the instant the obligatory handshake breaks, I thought, I'll bombard him. Overwhelm him with questions. I'll be in his face before he ever sits his arrogant ass down.

But he was already in situ when I got there. Sitting by the window. Waiting. He folded his newspaper away and beckoned me towards his table with a twitch of his fingers.

'Have a seat,' he said. He did not offer his hand and bridged the awkward transition from meet to greet by glancing over my shoulder and catching Terri Carlson's eye. He indicated another coffee for himself, with the flick of an eyebrow. The implicitness of the communication demonstrated that I was still on his turf; *same again, the usual, my usual,* was what it said, or some other cosy nuance of small-town life that could either envelop or ostracise on the capricious design of the sayer.

His coffee arrived promptly and the young waiter enquired after my needs, though only on Novak's nod.

'A water. Still,' I told him.

'No coffee? Tea?' Novak asked.

'No, thanks. I don't expect this to take too long.'

Novak looked as he had on our first meeting; long-limbed—too long for the coffeehouse chairs and small tables—gauntly handsome, and refined.

'I've listened to Mr. Jackson's account. Several times, as you'd expect. And read what he wrote. And, as you know by now, I've typed up my own transcript. You received it, yes?' He nodded. 'I thought it might be helpful for you and Mr. Jackson to consider it before we go any further. So we don't waste each other's time.'

'Yes, Mr. Jackson is satisfied with the integrity of it. So far.'

'On that basis, then, I'll proceed.'

He nodded his head, again, but didn't speak.

'Since we last spoke I've also been interviewing some of the relevant witnesses. The student, Atley; some of Mr. Jackson's colleagues; a few of the officers concerned, Holmes and O'Connell, and the statement from Baros. There are a few more that I'd like to talk to too but so far I've been unable to get hold of. Ms. Quinn, most importantly, and Mr. Handy, maybe. I'd still like to talk with them. I'm trying to get a sense of what happened before and after the crime. Although the before of Mr. Jackson's crime, and the crime itself, are fairly comprehensively accounted for. From his side of things, at least. That said, I do have a few questions—regarding what I've put together so far—that might benefit from the attention of your expertise, Professor.'

The obsequiousness of my words embarrassed me but even as I sensed their artfulness I failed to repress them. The misplaced flattery was involuntary, a spasmodic seeking of impossible approval.

'Complete transparency,' he replied. 'Regarding the patient.'

His blunt aside laid out the terms of our discussion. Strictly. Any exchange between us was to be characterised by pragmatism and brevity. I breathed deep, placed my notepad on the table, wrote the date and a heading—Novak—and underlined it, and rallied as best I could. 'So Mr. Jackson's current state of mind then: is what he says reliable?' I asked, without looking up.

'Yes. As I've told you.' Novak looked out the window, following the steps of some passers-by on the pavement.

'But what kind of reasoning is behind it? I'm wondering why he's done this at all. Why tell anyone? What is the purpose? On a psychological level? Even from a legal perspective...'

'I'm not a psychologist,' he interjected. 'To be clear. I'm a psychiatrist. A doctor. My work is medical. And I'm certainly not a solicitor. So...' He allowed his reflex response to float between us, its unfinished rhetoric intended to mock any need I might have for further explanation.

'I appreciate the distinction you're making,' I replied. 'And I apologise,' I continued.

'To be clear,' he said. 'I don't do speculation. I can't. Won't allow it.'

'I understand. That's yours to give or withhold, as you see fit.'

'No,' he interjected again. 'It's not. It's not a matter of choice. This is what I'm telling you, I am not in possession of any other information other than what I have given you.'

'Sorry, I meant no...'

'Don't apologise. Your full attention will suffice.'

I was forced to pause again, so sharp was he. Then, dispensing with civility, I asked, 'What's he at here, Professor? Have you any explanation?'

'No.'

'You've no idea whatsoever why he's doing this?'

'No.'

'So what do I do then?'

'You talk to Mr. Jackson,' he responded, plainly.

'Well, that would be something. And in conversations between the two of you, may I ask, has he said anything that might need explanation or qualification? Before I get in there with him myself.'

'No.'

'So you're just the guy who writes up the meds? You've no other meaningful insight?'

'We've talked, of course we have. He's my patient. But I've nothing much to say.'

'So what do you think about what he's told you? Can you give me something more here?'

'No, I can't. Because it would carry no authority. It would be merely an opinion. A personal opinion. Entirely unscientific. I ask him questions and talk with him as a means of drawing out other information. And as a means of assessing his well-being. And to assure him.'

'Just bedside manner, really?'

'Bedside manner?' he repeated, suddenly smirking, finding some obscure pleasure in the expression. 'Yes, why not?'

I stopped short of audibly scoffing at Novak's readiness to accept sarcasm as compliment. But exasperated by his reticence, each question I posed was now coloured by the insistent thought that it was he who had sought out me. I lost my patience with him.

'Perhaps I interpreted what you said too literally. 'Complete transparency' I believe were your words. I mean, that's what you said, wasn't it?'

'No need for the smart alecary,' he responded. He lifted his coffee to his lips and held it just beneath his nose before speaking again. 'I have told you all that I know—in fact! Fact! You understand?'

'What exactly is the story with you people?'

'*You people?*' he responded.

'Yeah,' I said, putting my pen down. 'All I keep hearing from you is facts. Fucking facts! There are only two facts: Mrs. Jackson is dead and Mr. Jackson killed her. After that, we've just got variations on a theme. Can't you see that?'

I leaned in over my water, towards him, in a manner I was sure he had never known a younger man to do. 'The fact is that the facts won't cut it here, pal. And this small-town mentality isn't doing anyone any favours. To move on we're going to need a little conjecture. Some speculation as to what went on inside his head. An educated fucking guess!' I sat back and sipped my water. 'From somebody, and the most qualified somebody here is you.'

'So you understand, at least,' he said.

'Excuse me?'

'You see now why he needs you.'

I looked at him quizzically.

'I just hope you're good, that's all. For Mr. Jackson's sake,' he said, running the flat of his fingers up his cheek, against the grain, and back down till he held his hirsute chin pinched between his fingers and thumb. Distracted by illicit thoughts— thing non-factual, subjective hypotheses I was precluded from knowing—he sat and waited for what I apparently already understood to dawn on me.

'I'm the storyteller, is that it? The conjecture is to be mine. I'm to impose order.'

'To assemble the *facts*, firstly. Yes. And you shouldn't have any problem in that regard. I think you'll have observed that for yourself already,' he said. 'Then you'll need to put shape on it. That's your job.'

'To imaginatively reconstruct?'

'Yes. But also to bring a different set of eyes to it. Eyes that haven't grown up round here. Can't you see the necessity of that?'

'We all have skeletons, right? And in a small town like this? Sure, yeah, I get it. But you came looking for me, remember. And these facts you're so fond of, there's a limit to them. They go only so far. If you want a grown-up story here, I'm going to need more. A story that will reflect the fullest complications of what happened, that is capable of going beyond official records and documents, will require someone to start talking. You understand what I'm saying? This is *my* field of expertise now. If you want a story, then I'm going to need things like motive, and remorse. I'm going to need ...' I said, having lost my point three or four meanders back, '. . . to talk directly with him.'

'That can be arranged. As I've told you,' he said, beating out each word.

The last traces of irascibility dissolved from his voice as he spoke. He appeared suddenly drawn rather than equanimous and it dawned on me that perhaps I had misread him. It mightn't have been obnoxiousness, or egotism, but exhaustion. The issue, it seemed, wasn't chronic objectivity, it was that he had become helplessly entangled in the intimate devastation of the Jacksons.

We looked at each other.

'I have also been speaking with his daughter,' he then said, in a manner that belied the potential momentousness of the development. 'Abigail. She's willing to talk to you.' He wrote her number down on a corner of newspaper, tore it off and slid it across.

'There's a son too, isn't there?' I threw in quickly.

'He won't talk,' Novak stated, and opened his wallet. He placed some notes in the dish in the middle of the table, enough to cover his coffees and a generous tip. Then he stood, vertiginously above me, and, for the first time, offered me his hand. 'I'll let you know about Mr. Jackson. Give me a couple of days,' he said.

The daughter: Abigail Jackson

ABIGAIL JACKSON WAS twenty-one, almost twenty-two, when her father murdered her mother.

During our introductory phone conversation she was polite and to the point, agreeing to meet me but only in a neighbouring town. She was understandably wary of the attention her return might draw. The arrangement made, she said goodbye and hung up.

I can't remember what exactly I had expected but the demure perfection of her standing in a mauve, pleated skirt to her knee, and a simple white blouse, her auburn hair billowing onto her shoulders, made me consider, among many other things, throwing myself in the ocean; in honour of her unadorned beauty. Her voice, soft and thoughtful, was immixed with sorrowfulness. What was alluring in her was inseparable from tragedy.

I arrived on the eleven o'clock train. In my jeans and casual wind sheeter I was conspicuous among the dozen or so passengers who disembarked; a melancholy legion of elderlies, sloping off at random stops, on journeys devoid of purpose. She identified me immediately among these mid-morning vagabonds and pensioners and I had my hand outstretched from ten yards away as she held me in her gaze. Out of courtesy, and a desire not to be over-familiar, I addressed her several times in the next few minutes as Ms. Jackson, and was halted on each occasion. 'Abi will do nicely enough. Under the circumstances.'

I asked her if she'd like to sit down, over coffee. But she wanted to walk. 'Along the promenade. Down to the West Pier. I like it there. There's something about water, don't you think?'

She smiled warmly at her own observation, taking from her handbag some cigarettes and lighting one. The sun crackled between the mottled clouds above, finding stretches of blue and shining brilliantly for a few minutes at a time before dimming out behind the gauze of intermittent cloud.

We didn't say much at first, and walked at such a languid pace that we could have been confused for two people who had known each other for many years. In the easy weave of it, I found myself imagining us hand in hand; our eyes meeting as we walked, across our shoulders, regarding each other with a misplaced but reciprocal fondness. I felt an inexplicable familiarity tacking between us; something more than relative contemporaneity.

'So you should start,' she said.

With the sun at her back, her face was bathed in soft shadows, and a sassy tilt of her hips thrust one shoulder provocatively forward, presenting me with the vigour of her half-turned face. A chunky stone necklace of turquoise, blacks, brown and grey-tinged whites, rested on her chest, and heaved slightly upward with each inhalation of her cigarette before sinking delicately back into the flesh, as she exhaled.

I gestured her onward with my hand and tried to think how to start, taking one last glance at the fullness of her peachy lips, shimmering in a light coat of pinkish-red gloss.

'Your father—have you seen him?'

She took a breath. 'No. Though I have tried. But he won't allow it.'

'But you want to see him?'

'Not really. But I thought I should.'

'Why?'

'I assume certain things, I suppose.'

'Like what?'

'Mental illness, I think. Rather than ... who knows?'

'Do you believe that?'

'I don't know what I believe. I've spoken with Professor Novak, of course. But I don't know. I just thought Dad deserved the chance to explain.'

'That seems extraordinarily empathetic,' I suggested.

'Extraordinarily.'

'You don't believe me?'

'It's more that I don't understand.'

'I love my father too,' she insisted, with strained poise.

Who she loved—once, always, forever, no more—I had never intended to broach. Her feelings for her father were her own, as far as I was concerned. I had no intention of passing judgement on them and that unimaginable conflict. But she had, by bookending her response with that unsolicited adverb, and doing so with such keen emphasis upon it, raised an issue whose power of intrigue would not be easily quelled.

'He killed your mother,' I said. 'How do you ever resolve that?'

'He was a good man,' she said, suddenly. 'And we were close. I still remember that. It's not as easy as picking sides.'

'Does your brother feel the same?'

'Of course not. And I'd expect nothing less. He has always been so full of surety. I am the one who finds liberal greynesses in those he'd rather execute.'

'So he thinks...'

'No,' she stopped me. 'He's said nothing of the sort. He's just much more straightforward than me, that's all I'm saying. And more reliable, therefore,' she added, attempting to burn-off any potential for her assessment of her brother to be perceived as antagonistic.

'More reliable?'

'In many respects, yes.'

'So am I not to trust what you tell me then?'

She smiled. 'It may be more multifaceted is what I'm saying. Or just confusing maybe.' She paused. 'Jake has no great passion for motive. For looking back ways. He's all about what's in front of us. So, no, I'm not suggesting I possess greater intellect, or even a broader perspective. I'm just saying that I don't expect a consensus.'

'Is one needed?'

'I'm not sure. Do you think you'll be needing one?'

I laughed at how far out of my depth I was.

'What do you think all this will achieve?' she asked.

'I haven't a clue,' I told her. 'I'm not sure it can achieve any-thing. The truth is that your father, or Novak, has hired me. And, frankly, I need the money.'

'I appreciate your honesty, Mr. Vaughan.'

'Charlie, please.'

'Yes, Charlie, of course. Well, Professor Novak has gone beyond the call of duty here, I think. It will be my father's—my parents' estate—that pays your fee though. I promise you that you will see that payment promptly. I will do my best to see to that.'

'And what's Novak's role in all this? It seems to be more than just a clinician.'

'Another good man, Charlie. There is some debt of gratitude between them. It goes back years. But I don't know the details. Just that the Professor and my father have known each other a long time.'

'Friends?'

'Yes, I think so. But not in the 'Come to dinner' kind of way. As a child I have memories of them stopping on the street in town to talk. Just a few words and walk on, but always cordial.'

'Well, that is at least a partial explanation. I've also been wondering though,' I began, 'what Novak has told you about me. About what he thinks my role in this could be?'

'He told us, simply, that my father wanted a writer to tell his story. He told us that my father had someone in mind. And now here you are.'

'Why me though?'

'Probably just because Dad had seen you about town, I'd imagine.'

Abigail Jackson's relationship with her father had been better than good. 'A loving father,' she said, pointedly, as if to evidence that everything wasn't black and white.

'I'd go further even,' she said. 'He was a really good man, loving. And he was influential. A funny word, I suppose. But he was, in so many ways. I'd go as far as to say that I think I learned everything good I know about men from my father.'

She paused so that I could ingest this, as if it was something

deeply absurd but no less real for being so. Looking out across
the sinewy water, narrowly rippling under the strain of ageless
contraction, I thought there were tears in her eyes, and permitted
her the conciliatory soliloquy.

'I heard somebody once who said that her brothers were the
barometer for all other men in her life. But mine was always
Dad. I measure everything against him. I see him sitting at the
table, his kind face reflecting back at me. That's what I see when I
think of him. And what I'm amazed by, although I'm sure I never
even thought about this until now, is that I can't hear his voice.
I just see him. Always smiling. Laughing quietly at whatever I
told him. But I can hardly remember a single thing he ever said
to me. Of course I don't mean he never spoke to me, I mean that
when I think of Dad what I see is his face. Relaxed—and gentle,
so gentle—looking back at me. At that table. But I don't know
that we ever actually talked in that time. What was between us
was something else. And now that I see that, of course, I can
see, too, where some of the tension between Jake and Dad might
have come from. I never remember Jake at that table with us.
Ate his food and left. For the TV or his friends. Or football. But
me and Dad remained. At the time … I was just a kid. But now,
when I think of it, I wonder … Perhaps I'm blowing it up bigger
than it was, remembering things wrongly.'

We were still walking, though we had slowed considerably.
She shook her head, irritated suddenly, by herself, perhaps, by
whatever had allowed her to ramble.

'What I'm trying to say is … You want to know about Dad,
right? Well, all I can give you is my impression of him. Because
that's all any of us have of anybody, right? My father stood
over me all my life—protecting me. Smiling me onward. My
impression of him, for some reason, is informed by this recurring memory of us at our kitchen table. I don't know why. The
face I see looking back at me each time is the same one. It never
changes. But what I think is that there is a truth about our relationship, and that that image I've retained is its encapsulation.
I feel,' she said, an imminent change of intonation beginning
to shudder through her voice, 'that you should understand this

part before anything else I say. So that you will know it first. He was a good man, he really was. And I love him.'

Stopping, I offered her a napkin taken from some tables set up along the pier, beside an ice cream vendor. She dabbed her eyes, compressing the napkin under each one to soak up the tears, and wiped them away. 'I mean I hated him first. Of course I did. He's taken everything and turned it inside out. I seethed, really seethed. But the problem was that after months of that the only thing that actually made me feel any better was crying for him. I didn't understand. My emotions felt like someone else's. I'd like to hate him. Because I feel guilty for wanting to see him. For loving him. And for mum.'

For whatever reason, she appeared more beautiful to me at that moment than any other—weakened by grief and by the futility of what might have been in any other set of circumstances—and I struggled to remain focussed. I wanted to reach out and fill the void created by her father, wanted to protect her from torturous reflection and recriminations, from loss.

She began looking in her handbag then and as she rested her large sunglasses on the bridge of her nose, and flicked her hair from her shoulder, she sunk from view. The clean precision of her cool aesthetic, now concealed behind dark lenses, svelte-like, and one degree too far from the reach of anyone's heart, depersonalised her.

'I'm not going to ask too much about your mother,' I declared, attempting to regain control of myself. 'Popular sentiment will take care of her. But my job is your father's story. Can I ask more about him? About him and your mother?'

She glanced out to sea and said, 'Why not?'

'Their relationship—how was it?'

'That's quite broad, isn't it?'

'I'll localise and narrow down as we go.'

'I don't know what to say. How does anyone answer that?'

'Impressions. Back to impressions. If you had to pick a few words to describe it, what would they be? Start there, maybe.'

'I don't know what to say, I really don't.'

'Were they happy?' I asked.

'I don't think so,' she said. 'Is anyone?'

'So were they unhappy then?'

'They were *comfortable*,' she said, labouring slightly over the word. 'Comfortable with each other. Their worlds and the various irritations they caused each other seemed to fit quite comfortably together. I can't imagine them apart.'

'Did they ever fight?'

'Physically? Absolutely never. There's not a trace of violence in my father,' she said, and we both allowed the obvious to slide so as to spare her train of thought. 'In fact, my mother herself used to joke that he was so much more than just a pacifist—he was an impassivist, she would say. He had his passions though. It was just that the things that possessed him weren't visible. He got drawn into things, became owned by them. When he was reading, he just didn't hear you. Or if something was irritating him, he just didn't know how to conceal it. Or ignore it. You'd see him fidgeting about you, or pacing or muttering. But there was never any physical threat though. None. Anybody else will tell you the same.'

'But they argued?'

'Like any married couple of twenty-five years. They bickered. They were so wrapped up in each other for so long that they could neither be together nor apart. They annoyed each other as part of their everyday routine. You know, just like anyone, really. Which way the toilet roll hung on the roller—inways or outways. Whether butter was kept in the fridge or out. Or Mum's resenting that he never thanked her for ironing his shirts. As a matter of manners. And him claiming he didn't care if they were ironed or not. Even though we all knew he'd have been a quivering wreck if he'd ever had to step out the door in a creased shirt. Or the garden! His hatred for it. They argued all the time, spring through summer, every year, about how pointless a job it was and the drama he always made of it. He'd argue that it was work that never ended, and she'd compare it to his shirts and trousers. And then there'd be an embittered and disingenuous truce, claiming that neither of them cared about 'the fucking garden' anyway, and it would go untended for a month. Until somebody would be coming over for dinner. And all of a sudden Dad would be found—before Mum even said anything—out weeding, strimming, mowing. Because the truth was that he wanted it kept too. But halfway through the job, he'd be standing in the kitchen, giving out to the air that it was a 'bloody nightmare' when you left it so long, and it was a job he'd never asked for. The stuff of any family, I suppose.'

We walked on a little further until we reached the end of the pier. There were several blue-painted benches, wooden and backless, facing out into the harbour, and we sat down. Although physically close on the bench, we were held apart by the sliver of sunlight between us, pushing and straining at its perimeters, filling up the space like expanding foam. We were side by side but demonstrably apart.

'Do you think she loved him?'

'Oh, absolutely. I think there was a part of her that simply adored him,' she said. The timbre of her voice changed, rising poignantly. 'And she was affectionate. Very tactile. Would run a hand across his shoulder as he sat at the table. Or across his face, looking up to him and straightening his jacket before he went out the door. And he'd pretend he was indifferent to it but he wasn't. He'd loiter by the hall table, pretending to look for something, to give her time to finish her make-up and get down the stairs and give him that wordless approval. And I think she knew he waited too. She'd drive him crazy because he could never ask for it, you see.'

In the same instant as she, I think, I noticed another tear dripping from the lower rim of her black glasses. Lodged between the rim and her velvet cheek for a moment or two, it fattened and distended, before bursting with celestial lightness into the thin neckline of her blouse.

'There was tremendous love between them, I know that. It wasn't showy. But it was there. Maybe you'd need to have hung around the place for a decade to have seen it. I think that maybe they appeared a bit rigid, or something, to other people. But they were hugely comfortable with each other, you know. There was real affection. That's what I remember.'

'When was the last time you saw them?'

'The month before. I'd been away all summer. Working. Came home for a few days in late August, before going back to Uni.'

'And there was no change between them? Nothing at all?'

'None. Genuinely. In fact, if somebody had asked I would have said that they had become slightly more comfortable with each other. But maybe it's just that they weren't speaking much. It's so hard to say now, to judge what I thought then. All I know is that I didn't notice anything. Perhaps I was too wrapped up in myself. I mean that's occurred to me too. I've wondered...'

She began then to openly weep and was forced to remove her sunglasses to dry her eyes. As we moved back down the pier, she began apologising for her imminent departure. 'Sorry, just realising the time. We should walk while we talk.'

The vigour of our conversation on the way back to the station waned, shifting gradually toward platitudes and tentativeness. It seemed laden with a kind of sudden regret, or a sorry awareness of inevitable conclusion, in the way a thrilling holiday full of new friends and romances might dwindle and die in its closing days.

Her glasses were back on and a certain sassiness in her step had returned by the time we reached the station. There were a few minutes to spare before her train departed so I walked her as far as the carriage door. On the platform, I thanked her for her time and her candidness. She put her hand on my elbow and leaned in to kiss me. Just before we brushed cheeks, and before I caught the fruity sharpness of her perfume, our eyes met through her darkened lenses and confirmed the atomic intimacies that had passed between us. In my ear, as her left hand reached lightly around my shoulder and rested on my back, she whispered, 'Thank you.'

For listening, I assumed. For caring, for her father, for the morning itself. And as she readied herself to go, I chanced one final question. 'Your brother, do you think he'd talk with me?'

'I doubt it,' she said, 'but I'll give you his number.'

She took her phone from her handbag and as we were saying goodbye Jacob Jackson's contact details beeped in on my phone.

She turned to board the train and wished me luck.

Afraid I might jump on the train and declare my love for her, right there and then, I turned away before the train had pulled out of the station.

I sat an hour over a coffee waiting on my own train. While sitting, I dialled Jacob Jackson's number. No answer. But heartened by my closeness to the family now, I left a message. Short and to the point. No bullshit. No schmoozing. This was serious stuff, I wanted to convey. Jacob Jackson was a formidable man, after all. Apparently. By reputation. And given what I'd learned of him, I was disinclined to pursue him too zealously. The casual message was sufficient. An almost flippant enquiry left on an answering service, it attested to no more than common courtesy.

The son: Jacob Jackson

ALTHOUGH WE WERE NEAR contemporaries, I had formed the impression that in comparison to Jacob Jackson I would come off as effetely boyish. His reputation trod before him, fending off insidious and earnest souls alike. But without him the project was at a kind of impasse, so I gambled everything on being straight with him.

I planned to tell Jacob what I had told Abigail, that I was just feeling my way through the story. I possessed no certainty at all as to where my efforts were headed. I knew what I wanted but not whether it would be of any use once I'd obtained it. All that was leading me onward was a faint but habitual narrative instinct. And that instinct had taken, in the days of silence between the left message and the terse return-call, to insisting that I could go no further without him.

This created a growing desperation as the days slid past. Irrespective of even the most paltry input on Jacob Jackson's part, even if it turned out to be, 'Fuck off and don't bother me again,' I needed it. I needed him to legitimise the project.

While the broad trajectory of the project had by then unfolded, the skeletal structure traced by Albert Jackson's very own strange account, added to the witness statements and his daughter's interview, now required something from Jacob Jackson too. Before I could proceed to the conclusion—an audience with Albert Jackson himself—I needed Jacob Jackson to say something to me. To write me. To email or text. To communicate through a third party, even.

So I waited those days, sitting on my hands, working on a number of other projects but never truly committing to them. Ostensibly content that there was nothing else that could be done.

But whatever endeavour I was fooling myself with, what I was really doing was waiting.

It was seven a.m. and I was still sleeping heavily. The day's inevitable disappointments and failures, the lot of an aspiring writer, had not yet been met when the phone woke me.

'Jake Jackson,' he snapped at me, as I put the phone to my ear. 'You left a message for me, yeah?'

I sat up and tried to find a pen and paper. Or my dictaphone. Anything that might salvage what would otherwise be lost to disorientation. 'Yeah, I ...'

'Well, what do you want?'

'Oh, well, it was in relation to...I talked with your sister, Abi, and she said...she gave me your number. So what I just...'

'You want something on my father, do you? Or my mother maybe?'

'Yes, but...'

'You're scum! You know that? Just what kind of sick fuck are you, anyway? And I've spoken to my sister too, actually, and I don't like it. Not one fucking bit. We're real fucking people, you understand!'

'I know, I know. I really do. I just...'

'An actual family. Do you get that? Can you conceive of it?'

'Of course.'

'What kind of a hack are you, eh? Some sick rag, is it? Looking for the inside scoop? Looking to sensationalise it all? A fucking murder! Death? Grieving? We're real bloody people, you understand!'

'I'm just a fiction writer,' I said, sitting up.

'So fucking what? Don't contact me again, you hear me? I'll have you arrested—you sick fuck!'

And he was gone.

Interviews with the patient: Albert Jackson

AWARE OF ALBERT JACKSON'S awful necessity, I edged onward. But I was afraid of him. I had admitted that much to myself before ever having met him. Afraid, in advance of any reality, of all aspects of how I imagined him. I feared the forthrightness of his son, feared it would prove a genetic trait of all Jackson males, and that in person Albert Jackson would intimidate me. And furthermore, that he would discredit and dismantle me with the very same conviction that had assured him I was what he needed in the first place. Upon meeting me, would that self-same conviction be inverted and would his disappointment find categorical assertion in some facial expression, or a moment of unguarded hesitation?

And there was, of course, that matter of him being a murderer. Thus far I hadn't been able to square that. An unidentified pressure, the product of conformity and conventionality, no doubt, tut-tutted at me all the way. In facilitating Jackson and his story, surely I had aligned myself with the wrong camp. As well as which, for me there was still something missing from his assorted statements. And it haunted my impression of him. Told me I was wrong to talk with him. The emotional hollow, the thin precision, the soulless control. What essence of him could be redeemed if the deadpan brutality of his murderous account proved as faithful as Novak had suggested it was?

Novak left me waiting a quarter of an hour.

'It would suit me fine if you had nothing more to do with the Jacksons,' he began, taking a seat opposite me, as he had on our first meeting. 'To be honest, and it's nothing personal, but I have continuously told my patient that he is not better yet. He will never be better. This is not advisable.'

With instinctive swiftness, I assured Novak that I'd endeavour not to take personally his immense intolerance of me. 'But,' I added, 'I'm interested that you say you've advised him against it.'

He looked at me, impatience flaring in the whites of his eyes. 'This is not a good idea, Mr. Vaughan. He doesn't need it. Doesn't need you. Who knows where this will go.'

'What do you want me to do here, Professor?'

'I want nothing,' he cut across me. 'If you wish to proceed, then do so. If you don't, so be it. I will gladly make your excuses.' I was about to interject when Novak excused himself. 'Now, I'll go about setting this event up. You will have two hours.'

'Two hours?' I asked.

'Yes, that should be sufficient. After that, we'll have to see. It's not just about him, I'll have to make a clinical decision too.'

Albert Jackson was waiting for me, dressed in a plain, open-necked, fitted shirt and trousers, and wearing some smart black shoes. He was sitting on one side of a small table, his back to a blank wall, and looking quietly out the expansive glass doors into a walled garden, criss-crossed by cobble-locked paving and a minimalist stone fountain at the centre. He turned and smiled as I entered.

'Mr. Jackson,' the attendant said, signalling my arrival.

'Thank you, Martin,' Mr. Jackson replied, as the door was pulled shut. His voice was soft and courteous. Not unfamiliar.

'Charles Vaughan,' I introduced myself.

'Yes, of course,' he said, standing up. But then his gaze fell away, to the side, as if he had been overcome by a sudden self-consciousness. He shuffled awkwardly on the soles of his shoes, illuminating what might otherwise have been an undetectable nervousness.

By the time I'd crossed the room to shake his hand he had reassumed a demeanour of polite confidence. In the smoothness of his face there was an agelessness, a deadened timelessness. A pair of quiet, green eyes flickered and shone above a mod-estly sleek nose. His hair was a little longer than I would have expected, having seen the understated dapperness of the rest of him. But perhaps, I thought, this was just for want of a barber.

'The gardens are beautiful here,' he said. 'The others erect bird tables, or work the flower beds. But I'm happy to just look out upon it. Never been much of a garden man, to be honest.'

'Yeah,' I said, 'it must be very pleasant to …' I couldn't finish my thought. 'That must leave you with a lot of time to think,' I said.

He snorted weakly. 'It does, indeed.'

I wanted to walk away. Turn and go. I wanted the door to open and save me from being swallowed by that room. But it felt too late for that. 'Novak says I have two hours. So I think we really need to dive straight in here,' I said.

'You're absolutely right. Sit down. This is no time for foreplay.'

It was hard not to identify the bitter vanity of the recordings echoing back at me as this peculiar choice of phrase thudded to the floor. His feet shuffled and scuffed the carpet, again, as he stood aside, patiently, allowing me space and time to ready myself. One thing was certain—what he said, and his reaction, proved that Albert Jackson comprehended cause and effect. He was not at that moment deranged, or insane. He was sentient, compos mentis, sufficiently in control of his faculties to know his own inappropriateness.

'The murder, Mr. Jackson,' I said. 'Why?'

He looked directly back at me, time stopping as the plainly penetrative question resonated in his eyes; swirling, tightening, moistening, steeling. 'Because I was unwell,' he stated, having considered the tone and tact of the question.

'My directness here is unfortunate,' I tried to explain, 'but it is the elephant in the room. I don't think there's much point in this, for either of us, unless we can come at it head-on.'

He bobbed his head, in reluctant agreement. 'I'm not sure why. Because that man is not me. He wasn't me.'

'Do you have any memory of the act?'

'The act? We can call it that, if you like. If it's easier for you,' he said, a sudden mocking in his voice.

'Why did you murder your wife, Mr. Jackson?'

'That's more like it, now,' he said, wringing his hands. 'I don't know exactly. I loved my wife. I genuinely…'

'So why did you kill her then?' I interrupted.

'I don't know.'

'I'm sorry for the directness, as I said. But time is against us.'

'I have no answer for that question.'

'Can you explain to me what went through your mind then? You were aware, obviously, that it was your wife in the bed as you reached out to kill her?'

'A touch simplistic,' he replied. 'I knew she was my wife but I couldn't feel it. My mind, my chest,' he said, rigidly cupping one hand below his chin, as if he held in it the purified essence of his distress, 'was heaving and caving in. My body knew what my mind was thinking was madness. But the mind raged. It was desperate. And the body? It just gave way. Timidity, and a poor habit of compliance, I suppose.' He fanned-out the trembling fingers of both hands, palms hovering barely above the table top. 'Everything was in the mind. The hands were guilty of nothing. *They* are not guilty. I thought it was the body acting alone, at first. This is what it felt like, but that just can't be. Can it? It has to have been the mind.'

'And where is the mind now? The mind that perpetrated the crime—where is it? How is it?'

'It is unlocked,' he said, reflectively. 'Laid open. But in the possession of Professor Novak,' he added with a playful smile.

'I'm afraid these abstractions won't get us very far? Would you like to start again?'

'Why am I here?'

'Because I read your book, Charlie. May I call you Charlie? Is that what you go by?'

'It is.'

'I liked your book.'

'I haven't exactly come here looking for validation.'

'Don't be embarrassed, Charlie,' he interrupted. 'This is no faint praise. I think it was a fine first novel. It is why I chose you.'

'What am I supposed to say to this?'

'Nothing. Just accept it. Your instincts are good. That's why

I looked for you. That and what I assumed would be a certain financial vulnerability. Struggling writers and all that. You're better than you think you are, Charlie.'

'Fine,' I said, palpitations in my chest as I tried to mediate between competing emotions. 'I'd like to focus again on the purpose here. What is it you expect?'

'Oh, that's simple enough. That's one I can answer with no ambiguity at all. I expect you to save me in the eyes of my children.'

I resisted laughter. Disbelieving laughter.

'I'd hoped Novak would have told you this already,' he said.

'This will open up the whole thing again. On you all. Have you considered that? What about the law? Public opinion?'

'The law?' he guffawed. 'What of it! I'm already guilty. And society, Charlie? Do you think that might still be up for grabs too? I think not. No, this is about the children. My children. I want them to know I'm not a monster.'

'I doubt they think that. They avert their eyes, probably. Turn away from thoughts of you, perhaps. Fairly understandable, I think.'

'But I want them to look. It is for them. My son and daughter. Although my son and I have not been close since he was a boy. Since he grew up. Since he realised that I hadn't invested much time in him; though I loved him more thoroughly than he will ever know... but such things are immeasurable. Whereas time... even if he doesn't have the precise figures to hand, he can still say with confidence that I invested virtually nothing in terms of time. It was naïve of me, in hindsight, to think he would just know that I loved him, to think it needn't be said. Needn't be demonstrated. But am I alone in that parental error, do you think?'

I moved to counter the fatuity of his sudden departure into the banalities of parenting but he stopped me, anticipating my response.

'But they haven't done what I've done, I realise,' he said. 'I digress,' he then offered, lightheartedly, before staring back into the face of it. 'I want them to understand I could never have done this to Val.'

Although I wanted desperately to pull the rug from the deluded and self-serving narrative he was attempting to put in play, with the obvious, 'But you did,' I withheld. It would have been too confrontational. Too true. For all his bombast, I still wasn't quite convinced of the resilience of his mind. 'Novak has explained all that to them, I'm sure.'

'Telling and showing are different things, though, aren't they? Which is why I need you. The novel as a paradigm, that's what I'm after. A working model of the lost mind,' he said, fixing me intently. 'To create empathy, of course. I'm aware that sympathy will never happen. Nor should it. But an understanding is what I'd like. Even if they never read it, I want the possibility to be alive to them. The clinical notes, theory, psychological what-have-yous; they only tell. They are restricted by their necessary form, and thwarted by the very objectivity that makes them credible. Blunt instruments, the tools of medicine and psychology. But the novel's a different beast entirely; pliable; capable of shifting and rolling with the fluctuations of the human heart, of clinging to the coattails of otherwise elusive patterns of the mind. It has range, human capacity, like nothing else.'

'You think highly of it, Mr. Jackson. But too highly, I suspect. And certainly too highly of me if what you are thinking is that I can make it perform such tricks.'

'Perhaps,' he said. 'But you are here, and as such you're all I've got. So shall we begin? Again.'

He began to talk then, rambling, taking in an array of inanities—the gardens, the birds, the food, the weather, the air-con.

I left him to talk freely, looking him over more closely as he spoke. I wondered whether or not he realised a loose thread hung from one of his shirt buttons. A man like this. So neat and precise. I imagined him unwilling to just pull the thread, wanting to sever it cleanly and correctly for fear of losing the button altogether. Was he waiting on a scissors, or Novak's permission for an attendant to cut it for him, I speculated, when he took an abrupt turn directly back into the meat of the issue.

'I loved Valerie. Val,' he declared. 'Novak tells me I should try to use her name and so I will, though it hurts to do so. There

is a sense in which I feel I have no right to use her name, especially not with the affection that is inherent when I say it. I'm
afraid it will seem disingenuous, or that my using her name, as
though she was still my wife, will be some kind of confirmation
of predetermined evilness, or assumed malignancy. I'm not evil
though. I don't think I am. I was sick ... I am sick. Still. In that
I cannot possibly not be here. I couldn't wake outside the walls
of this place.'

His throat begun to crackle, sanded dry by the thoughts free-
wheeling apace from inside, or the consequence of projecting
his voice after the lengthy months of contemplative silence. I
diffused the moment by stretching across and filling his glass
from the chrome decanter of water between us.

'Where were we? Yes, I remember. I loved my wife. That is
irrefutable, Charlie. I love my wife. And I love my children.'

'So why have you not allowed your daughter to visit?'

'You have spoken with her?' he asked.

'I have.'

'I'm biased, obviously, but she's something else, Charlie, isn't
she?' He beamed at the thought of her, then suddenly soured. 'I
won't ever see them again. It is for precisely this reason I need you.'

'Even though they want to see you?'

'Jake will never want to see me. I know that. He might want
to kill me, but not visit. There will be no visits.'

'So you do understand, completely, what you have done? The
impact, the devastation?'

'I comprehend the gravity of what I have done, yes.
Completely. And I should add that the gravity of that knowledge
is with me constantly. Passing through me. The love I have for
them and what I've done to them; a painful juxtaposition. It's
with me every day. And worsens as I get stronger, as my mind
comes back to me. And the time between the episodes of revis-
iting becomes less and less; like contractions. As if my mind is
readying itself for the birth of something terrible.'

He was quiet then as he considered what it was he meant.
He seemed constantly in search of words and images to explain
what he had only a feeling for.

'I see her face. That last image is the only one of Val I can con-
jure.' His voice had become flat, and his eyes dopey; the spoken
truth, the reality uttered aloud, had to be calibrated, controlled,
so that it wouldn't rupture and flush out with it what was left
of life's worth. 'Although the face I see on her body, bloodied
as it is, is not her final face. I see her as I saw her when we were
young. One of our first dates, maybe. Or some night when we, a
few long forgotten friends of mine and hers, who I can see now
but scarcely name, have gathered together. It's odd, isn't it, how
easily we let all those people go?'

I could muster no response, no insightful quip or follow-up,
and my inaction prompted him to continue.

'But the face she wears, in this recurring image, is not the one
I... I see her in the full of her youth. Almost baby-faced. Her
skin soft and tight. Her smile just so. Different each time, not
like the thing we cultivate as we get older. That's the face I see but
it is always in the final scene, you understand? Always covered
in blood. And wet, tangled hair. And it's starting to become a
matter of urgent seriousness. I'm living with it. I think I'm beginning to realise that. Which, long-term, is unfeasible. That may be
where Novak is coming from. I cannot go back out there, or into
some kind of detention centre, with things as they are. Novak
must cover himself, you see. And I don't say that with any sort
of acerbity, but more to try and show you that all is not what it
seems. Motivation is a complex animal. Expressed in a singular
form but many-headed. Forged simultaneously in the weakness
of the conscious mind and the chaos of the subconscious. And
which one governs it at the moment of perpetration, Charlie,
is no more than a matter of chance. I swear to you. And we all
have our own demons. In that sense, we're not all that different.
Any of us,' he said, with an upward glance.

He paused and thought. 'It was as if a mist, or a fog, had
lifted. Clichéd, yes,' he said. 'I see you turning up your eyes at
that one, Charlie. But never the less... Once I'd done what I'd
done and it had moved from misguided fantasy to reality, this
fog dispersed. That clarity, though, was not immediate. It only
really came about when I woke up here. After my work with the

professor had begun ... It had descended, this fog, it had been descending over I don't know how long, but I could not perceive any of it in reality. Not really. But the moment events passed into the irrevocable, the fog began to disperse. Or recede... What I'd do for that fog never to have lifted, never to have allowed me a clear vista over what I'd done. To be able to live out my days in some insane world of half-truths and fantasies ... We, myself and Val and all the people around us, became a kind of fiction to me, unreal yet intimately involved. I knew that she was my wife and I loved her while also knowing that I would do anything to clear the way for somebody else. For me to be somebody else. I could look at her and see both women at once. The woman I married and loved and the woman I needed gone.'

'Yes,' I interrupted, having recovered my bearings slightly and begun to frantically take notes, in an effort to map the tangential fancies of his thinking. 'That's something I'd like to ask about. The somebody else? Aimeé Quinn?'

His nerve dipped drastically at the mention of her name and he took several minutes to compose himself.

'It is one of the great pities of all this that Aimeé has been unavoidably ensnared in it.'

'It was hardly unavoidable.'

'My narrative required full disclosure. To be of any value, and unfortunately that meant her too. But Aimeé is a sweet young woman and she deserves far better than all this.'

'I apologise for this, Mr. Jackson, but I have to ask - did you ever have any relationship with her?'

'I did not! Colleagues. Nothing more. I can't be clearer about this—there was *nothing* between me and Aimeé Quinn. Other than what existed in my delusions. She is entirely innocent.'

'You're quite defensive, for a man who had nothing to do with her.'

'Mr. Vaughan, if there is one area of life where we should take care to be righteous, it is with the innocent. I want to dispel any notion that Aimeé Quinn could have been in any conceivable way a motive for my crime.'

'I ask because I've not yet had the opportunity to talk with her.'

'There's no need. And I would ask that you don't. She will know nothing of worth because it was all in my mind. Leave her alone, please.'

'So there was nothing between you? Nothing at all?'

'Absolutely. I give you my word.'

'And between her and Jones?'

'That I can't say.'

'But you were jealous of Jones?'

'Look, I don't like Jones, that much is true, but I can no more blame him than I can Aimeé. Unfortunately.'

He folded his arms and looked across at me.

'Okay,' I said, looking down at my notes. 'Fair enough. Let us return to you and your account. You were saying, about the moment of murder, about being aware but not aware.'

'Yes. That's correct,' he said.

'Can you expand on that a little?'

'I was somebody else,' he said, opening up again as if the entire exchange about Quinn and Jones had never happened. 'In that final moment. In fact, I was two people. What I'd like to know is why the real one didn't intercede. That's a question for Novak, I imagine. For him and his colleagues to pore over and apply their conceptual frameworks. In the days running up to it I was barely myself at all. I acted against Val in the midst of that fog. I acted against the entire reality of my life. It's unfathomable, even for me. This is what I kept telling Novak. When I woke up here, when I first could think, I wished to die. To be allowed death's release. I refused food and water. How could anyone ever make any sense of it? I asked. How could it ever be resolved? But I got stronger. More able to face myself. More willing. But as the weeks, the months now, have passed, I have begun to feel this frustration with the inadequacies of theory and conversation. With the people in here, and how they fail to grasp the impossibleness of the object they are probing. I found myself continuously resorting to narrative, at which point, inevitably, I'd be interrupted by their clinical observations. Then, several weeks ago, it struck me. A narrative, utterly candid and unafraid, is my only means of explaining. Novak needed much convincing, of course, just to get us this far. But I made it clear to him that I understood the risks. He's stubborn though. He resisted. Tried to dissuade me. He's afraid of what I'll be after the process. He fears it might be a dying wish; its hope keeping me alive and its realisation killing me. But I have persisted, even as he objects. He points out that there is no telling how the things I might say could be misconstrued. But I know that a narrative is the only hope of anyone else ever understanding. The account I'd already provided upon arrest, of course, was exactly that. The thing I was thinking of. Or part of it. And to think I've been working on it years without ever knowing. The fiction of my life.'

'So you had this prepared? Rehearsed? These accounts, do they pre-date the murder?' I asked, shocked by the idea. 'Were they written down somewhere? In advance of what happened?'

'You're surprised by that?'

'By the fact that you wrote your confession in advance? Yeah, it suggests an altogether different level of premeditation—quite obviously.'

'I hadn't thought of it like that. Just goes to show, we really don't have much control over how this will play out. But never the less, I must take that chance. So, yes, it was well-rehearsed. In so many ways. Most of it, at least. And it was written down too, but not anywhere you could find it. It's a product of a thousand soliloquys of the mind, random doodles on the back of notebooks or loose sheets of paper. The written element is scattered throughout the years - in bins, crumpled up in balls or torn to pieces. Stylised cameos of the man I thought I might be. If you could round-up all that pulp, you just might have it, I'd say. But it was all part of the rehearsal, as you put it. A narrative I'd been unwittingly working on my whole adult life. The accounts I have provided are not exactly verbatim, as such, you see. They weren't purely improvised. In many respects, I'd put a lot of time and effort into their construction. Indirectly. Does this help you?' he then asked.

'It goes some way to explaining the lucidity of it.'

'Well, that's something. I know, myself, that however stark my future is, any existing hope lies there—in the fact that what

happened can at least be told. And therefore laid open to inter-
pretation. By Abi and Jake.'

Mr. Jackson suddenly ceased to speak and I followed his eyes
over my shoulder to where the door had silently opened.

'I'm afraid you'll have to finish up a little earlier than expected,
Mr. Vaughan,' said the attendant, from the doorway. 'Professor
Novak sends his apologies.'

'We're supposed to have another forty-five minutes.'

'Professor Novak sends his apologies, as I've said, Sir.'

The hand on my shoulder was not cold or strong, but it left
my heart on the floor.

'It's okay. I'll talk with Novak. Come again. Tomorrow,' Mr.
Jackson said.

He then proceeded to walk to the door, past the attendant,
thanking him as he went.

'I can see him again tomorrow, right?' I asked.

'You'll need to clear that with Professor Novak, Sir,' the attendant responded.

'I was told I'd have access.'

'Like I say, Sir, you'll have to talk with Professor Novak.'

'Can I see Novak now? Before I leave?'

'I'm sure that's a possibility. Try at reception.'

I waited patiently at reception and by the time he arrived I was
well prepared.

'My apologies, Mr. Vaughan,' he said. 'I couldn't get away any
sooner. The work we do here is almost always urgent. No room
for postponement, I'm afraid.'

'Why was our meeting cut short?'

'Clinical reasons.'

'Could you be more precise?'

'No, I cannot.'

'But I can return again tomorrow?'

'I expect so, yes.'

'You expect so?'

'Yes. We have your number, we'll call you in the morning.'

'I could use something more concrete than that, to be honest.'

'I appreciate that, Mr. Vaughan, but Mr. Jackson's condition is precarious. Our only concern in this regard is his well-being. It wouldn't be judicious of us to proceed with a process as unconventional as this without having the necessary checks and balances in place. You understand, I'm sure.'

'Of course, but one of the conditions of my taking part in this was that I would have full access to the patient.'

'With the greatest of respect,' he said, sliding his hands into his trouser pockets and slouching back into his shoulders with elaborate disinterest, 'I'm not sure you're in a position to be placing any conditions on anything with regard to Mr. Jackson.'

'You promised me access! I'm after wasting weeks on this.'

He half grinned. 'If you wouldn't mind keeping your voice down, Mr. Vaughan. I'm doing all I can. If you can't return, I can inform Mr. Jackson that you were unavoidably called away. Required elsewhere. A personal matter, I can tell him.'

'He asked me to come back. Wants to speak to me again. And you'll make sure that's recorded in his notes, of course,' I said, already walking for the door, wagging my finger blindly over my shoulder. 'Tomorrow, Novak. See you tomorrow.'

I drove out of the Reil and straight into town, parked, and went to a bar. An uneven distribution of customers, mainly men, clustered in twos or threes, others alone, were tucked into the booths that skirted the trellis tables and seats that filled the hard floor—a dance floor on weekend nights—at the centre of the room. At the bar, there were two men sat at a corner and a barmaid on her break. Music droned low from the speakers on the walls, and from the wide muted screens sports and news flickered; flashing, breaking in manic red banners.

I downed a beer and ordered another. Obscured in the half-light, I leafed through the file I had been amassing, still with the presence of Albert Jackson's hand on my shoulder. I began to live inside the afternoon's experience; to feel the shape of it, and understand what it was I had.

I became convinced that Albert Jackson's humanity lay not with knowing him, or in the facts, but in the integrity of his confession. It would be the narrative depths that haemorrhaged up from between the lines of that confession that would reveal him, make a man not a monster of him—even as it hung and quartered him. But it had to be a full confession, I realised, one that incorporated the missing hours. Why these hours had been omitted in the first place I didn't know. Perhaps he was afraid, feared that the rest of his story wouldn't draw him in any kinder a light. Meeting him in person certainly hadn't suborned any feeling of warmth. There was no wounded man to be discovered in his eyes, nothing sympathetic or humbled or regretful. Just somebody deeply troubled, vulnerable and arrogant by turns. In person, he would convince no one—not a judge, not a jury, not the gossips on the street. No one would take the time to get beyond his lofty rhetoric.

I needed the missing six hours now. Simple as that. Hours during which he wrapped her up, transported her to the beach, and waited to be picked up. The story he wanted me to tell remained unanchored because it had no end in mind. It needed its aftermath—his guilt and shame, fear and panic.

Five beers and a belly of food later, with *Sweet Virginia* warbling in my ears like a lonesome cowboy, I was tired and getting on toward drunk. I gave up on it, closing the file over and binding it shut with an elastic band. I consigned it to my bag and set myself the task of not thinking about it. About him. Actively tried not to think any more about him. I became suddenly sleepy. Exhausted.

I called a taxi.

As it weaved along the roads outside the town the rain came down, a hypnotic paradiddle on the roof of the car. The passing trees melted into nothing as I stared out the window through the downpour. Beyond the bulbous clots of rainwater streaming down the windscreen it was not possible to see. But I kept on looking. Until the taxi came to a stop.

I was still awake an hour after getting home and the file was still in my bag but my thoughts had begun again to circle the matter of Albert Jackson. 'The weakness of the liberal mind is its failure to resist the solicitations of natural justice,' I read. A handwritten quotation on a single page in a notepad I kept. The notepad was spilling over with random quotations, references and statements I had been saving up since my college days. This one was accompanied by what appeared to be a page reference—59—but nothing else. I had read it some place and wondered what it meant and what I might do with it, years before I'd ever had a sniff of Albert Jackson. Now, I thought I might know. On a loose sheet of paper, I quickly copied the quotation out and beneath it I wrote … *While in times of personal struggle and shame we may be grateful for the ear of a bleeding heart, when a father murders a mother, when a husband bludgeons his wife, people tend to want blood. That's what Albert Jackson is up against. People want culprits, more than they want victims even, and in pursuit of those culprits they demand to see the deployment of a simple assortment of facts— the evidence—and an unambiguous sentencing. The simplicity of the sentence must be proportionate to the simplicity of the charges laid down; an eye for an eye; simple as. Albert Jackson knew well that for those on the sidelines, murder is murder, and nobody's going to step forward and say, 'Hang on here, ladies and gentlemen. All is not what it seems. Why don't we take a moment to root around in the margins and see what turns up …*

I thought this might eventually make a prologue of sorts. It is one of countless notes and addendums that were written in the margins along the way, and although the essence of the project murmured at me through those lines, they were merely *saying* when the art was in *evoking*. Or *showing*, as Albert Jackson had put it.

For the first time I felt as if I was fully accepting of my brief. I would appropriate the narrative form provided, take its inherent convolution and dig deep into Albert Jackson's soul. A pseudo-fiction, that's what I'd dish up. Something that could unstick the stodgily compacted fusion of fact and fantasy that peppered his account, and run the arc of those two narratives side by side, long enough for them to be observed intersecting. Then, maybe, if it was good enough, it could unravel motive and intent in a manner so tragic that it would deflect from the heinousness of the crime.

Maybe he is right, I thought. The novel might just be the only thing that can plead on his behalf. It could plead for clemency on grounds of the heart's impossible vagaries. The heart - that would be the story. That he had one.

It was ten-thirty a.m., precisely, when an attendant came to show me to the room. Mr. Jackson was waiting for me, and Novak was at the table with him.

'Good morning,' I said.

Mr. Jackson stood up to greet me.

'And morning to you too, Novak,' I then said. 'You were supposed to call me. To confirm. But no matter. How long have I got?'

'*Professor Novak*,' he retorted, returning his attention to Mr. Jackson. 'Okay, Albert. We'll talk afterwards.' Then he turned back to me. 'And we too must talk, Mr. Vaughan. Afterwards.'

'Why not,' I said. 'Now how long have I got?'

'We'll see.'

'You're a rude bastard, Novak, you know that?'

Mr. Jackson peered out at the birds in the garden and the bright morning that slanted across it. His clothes were neat and ordered, as before. He gave forth steadiness and confidence. And a slightly disconcerting stillness.

'So, are you ready to begin?'

He turned and smiled, inviting me to continue.

'How were you yesterday?' I asked. 'After our session?'

'Professor Novak will tell you he is concerned, but he doesn't fully understand. As we do. But I'm fine, thank you. I'm pleased that you've returned. Professor Novak is capable of great kindness, but he is also bloody-minded.'

I waved his defence of Novak away, as if it weren't required. 'I'd like to start with what you just said. Or implied. That I *understand*. I'm not sure I do, Mr. Jackson. To be honest.'

'You will see in time that you're feeling for my case, while largely instinctive, is sound,' he replied as if he'd been expecting the question all along.

'How can you know that?'

'I can tell. From what you've done so far.'

'I have some very plain questions to put to you,' I said, eager to start and get finished. 'Direct and uncomplicated. But I must insist you provide answers to them. Full and frank.'

'Whatever you like. I'm ready. More ready than ever, in fact. Proceed. No holds barred.'

'Why should I be giving voice to a murderer?'

He shifted in his chair. 'We've been through a bit of this already, of course, but ...'

'Well, yes, but I'd like to put the theoretical aside, if you don't mind. For my own peace of mind, in terms of basic human decency—morality, if you like—why do you deserve a voice?'

'I see we've dispensed with the refinements, the fluff, Charlie,' he said, and my spine quivered at the renewed familiarity. 'And that's just fine. Why? you ask. Because I'm trying to help the victims here ... My son. And my daughter. In particular.'

'Both your son and daughter, in particular, or your son and, in particular, your daughter?' I asked, needlessly provoking him.

'Both!' he snapped, but then settled quickly back into his chair. He breathed in through his nose and released evenly. 'This is my only chance to put things right, Charlie. And the window of opportunity will not remain open indefinitely. These relationships are not ... they ...'

'They're up for grabs, Mr. Jackson, to use your own expression,' skimming theatrically over my notes with my finger.

He looked at me, resolutely, calming himself. 'I love my son and daughter. And I love my wife, Charlie.'

'Loved,' I interjected, and he stopped. 'So my questions then?' I paused. 'What I want to know is what you thought as you looked at your wife, dead in the bed?'

He was breathing heavier and glaring into me. 'My memory here is not too good. My thoughts were scattered afterwards.'

'How did you feel?'

'I can't say. I just don't know. I've already told all I know of what I did.'

'I don't believe that, Mr. Jackson. And more to the point, this project can't continue without something more.'

'There's nothing I can tell you?'

'We'll park it then. For now,' I said. 'How about another question?'

'By all means,' he said, elaborately ingratiating.

'Why didn't you hand yourself in?'

'I would say that I did. More or less.'

'I would say that you wrapped your wife's body up and tried to dump her in the sea. And I would say that that is far from handing one's self in. How about another question?' I asked but didn't wait for his imprimatur. 'How did you spend the next six hours after you bludgeoned her?'

'I'm not sure. I told you.'

'But what about the kids, Mr. Jackson? How is it we are going to help them when you're not prepared to be honest with them?'

'I recognise,' he said slowly, 'that the fallout here is immense. Sincerely, I do. I understand that ...'

'I can't help feeling that you don't. You don't understand.'

'I do,' he said. 'I've been open about this, Mr. Vaughan, the only ones I'm concerned about here are my children.'

'And yourself.'

'This is not for me. I think you know that.'

'What makes you think I understand anything about you, Mr. Jackson? You talk of people knowing, the need for people to know, to *understand*, Mr. Jackson, as if you've decided to resign from the parents' council or something. You murdered your wife! Your children are victims of this, indeed. But there are other victims too. Many of them. Your wife, for example. She's the chief victim. Nobody has been more victimised in all of this. You keep banging on about other people's *understanding*, Mr. Jackson, but where's yours?'

He sat back into his chair, rested his hands on his lap, and considered me. 'I expected this, of course. I had to. You must be concerned for your own reputation here. I'd hoped it wouldn't deteriorate like this. But I knew it might. The question for us now—at this point, Charlie, because you seem to have lost your cool and your objectivity with it—is are you prepared to go on? I am. Even in hostility. Even in fear. Are you?'

'If you answer the questions! Straight answers.'

'If you ask me a question, I'll answer it,' he said, leaning forward.

'What happened after you murdered her? Tell me what you did? How you did it? Tell me why?'

'I brought her to the beach. And I lay there with her,' he said, with no inflection.

'You can't do this,' I said. 'You can't pull back on me now. I have to know these things. The missing hours, you've got to be prepared to fill them in. Otherwise this won't work.'

'I brought her to the beach,' he said, softer this time, the cadences of his speech slipping closer to mantra than dialogue. 'And I lay with her there.'

'Your account ended with the second blow to her head. Is that when you realised? What did you do as you looked upon her dead body? Or was she even dead? Did she hang on in there for a few minutes? What happened? From beating her about the head to being picked up at dawn, what happened? You have to tell me what you did with those hours? One final disclosure. If you fail here it will throw doubt on the veracity of everything else.'

He got up from his seat and walked to the window. With his back to me, he stood silent.

Determined that the next words would be his, I waited. Sometimes staring at his back, ready to meet his eyes if he turned, sometimes staring into the corner of the room.

'I can't remember.'

'Can't remember anything?' I said, incredulously. 'I'll walk away, Mr. Jackson. I assure you.'

'I can't remember.'

'What are you afraid of? Now, at this stage? Jesus! With what you've said to date, what in the name of Christ could you be afraid of now? Talk! Speak to me! Or I'm leaving. '

'I can't remember,' he repeated.

'I'm done here,' I said, bundling my notes and equipment into my bag. 'You're withholding. You want understanding and integrity and balance. You want truth. Well, then everything has to come out, Mr. Jackson.'

His head rocked gently back and forth on his shoulders, his back still turned to me.

'But that's not what's happening here. This,' I opened up my palms and threw out my arms, looking around the room, 'this is bullshit. You can stick your commission!'

He looked round at me then but continued in his failure to respond. 'But I can't remember.'

Novak was waiting at reception.

'You've got what you want now, Novak,' I said walking straight past him.

'Mr. Vaughan?' he called out, after me.

I looked back over my shoulder, still in full stride away from the place, before stopping. Poised to set off again at any moment, I invited him to continue. 'What?'

He stood up from the counter, where he had been surveying and signing some documents, and stepped lankily across the foyer in my direction. 'Mr. Vaughan,' he repeated, 'while I have been short with you, I would like you to know that it is not personal. My concern is for my patient. Whatever has happened is beyond my control. But if it means that you are leaving and this idea can be put behind us, then I am pleased. I think it best for us all.'

'Yeah, good luck now,' I said, walking again.

My frustration carried on late into the evening. I tried to distract myself—watching TV, ordering some food, not eating it, typing a few lines onto the end of some unfinished manuscript that I still held vague aspirations of finishing, sending a few emails, watching some more TV. Eventually, in the earliest hours of the morning, I fell asleep.

I slept soundly but woke just before six a.m. and was unable to get back to sleep. Restless, I made tea and toast, dipping in and out of the TV news. Then I sat at my desk for a while, opened a series of documents on my laptop but managed to write nothing. I began to think about how, before I had undertaken the Albert Jackson project, that I had been dabbling in two other projects, jumping erratically from one to the other. I had been about forty-five thousand words into one and twenty into another. One, in particular, interested me, but it had been beached, with Albert Jackson's immovable insistence poised between me and it. I tried to get back to it but couldn't. Then, after a while, I returned to watching the TV from my bed.

Around nine, the morning haze cleared and I drove to the shore. En route, I daydreamt about how prolific I could be if only my own imaginings would stir such urgency in me. I continued to persuade myself, all the short way there, that this was possible, that one day my own words and creations would move me like the real lives of other people.

Down at the water, I dived headfirst into the frothy head of a just-breaking wave and the hollow soundlessness beneath the water encompassed me, flushing my senses through and suspending me in an opaque tranquillity. I moved in slow motion, breath held and arms sweeping, clawing mutedly through the clear ocean. I began to loosen up, the composite weight of events dissipating.

At intervals I allowed my head to pierce the still water's surface, beyond the breaking waves, and the soundlessness of submersion crashed gently in on itself. My head and shoulders bobbed atop the silky ripples. Then I floated on my back, looking upwards to the sky; cool, lazuline, faintly streaked by nondescript cloud. Some gulls circled and squawked, then flapped and fled. The swish of small waves in shallower water, fizzing up over the warming sand, were virtually all there was to hear. I wallowed, like a hippo in mud, in that moment of blissful promise that precedes the doing of any work; a time where potential vastly outstrips probable failure.

Shivering in my towel, I looked out across the sea and down the beach. I tried to imagine what Albert Jackson would have been thinking as he sat on the sand, holding the body of his dead wife between his legs, with the tide creeping slowly up the beach. I didn't know the precise spot, only that it would have been somewhere close to where I stood right at that moment. It had been earlier in the morning, of course, and the sea, the sand, the air would all have been cooler. Could he have been in his right mind then, just sitting there with her, waiting to be picked up? Could he have felt the coldness of early morning and the water and not been brought back to reality by it? Had he been frozen in fear? Or revulsion? Or in utter confusion? Could he really have appreciated what he'd done? Did he even remember? Why did he do it? How could he?

This is what I kept returning to. The awfulness of the crime was the hook but what people would want, consciously or otherwise, was an examination of how he felt afterwards. And how he gets through each day. Was he crazy, and if he was then but isn't now, how he lives with it?

Albert Jackson's account ceased right at the moment where the real interest lay. This was its shortcoming and I felt certain that the fault was his rather than any inadequacy of mine. Having promised everything, he had, at the crucial moment, withdrawn. I had no choice once he reneged. I had to walk away.

I dried myself off, dressed, and sat on the sand a while. Still looking out to sea. To see. Thinking of nothing.

On the drive home I began turning over a sentence in my mind. A new sentence. A paragraph starter. All promise, it was a tingling at the tips of my fingers. The start of something new, it might unlock me, I thought. In a matter of hours I would have momentum, and the frustrations of Albert Jackson and Novak and their veiled loyalty to each other would be old news.

But on the porch, waiting as I pulled in, was a man. Heavy-set, with a pleasant face. Wearing casual Chinos and trainers, and a loose-fitting check shirt, I couldn't quite place him until he stood up from the step. I turned off the engine and seeing the small brown parcel in his hands, I knew.

As with the initial parcel, this one was accompanied by a covering note:

Mr Vaughan,

Please find enclosed, at Mr Jackson's firm-
est insistence, one further revelation.
Hand-written. Not in the first person either but
the third! Any armchair psychologist could draw
conclusions from that. At any rate, it's yours
now. Use it as you see fit.
Martin will have delivered this and you should
know that he is trustable and discreet. I trust
you recognise that my patient's well-being is
what I've protected all along. I've advised
against what Mr Jackson is doing. What can it
achieve? But I'm obliged as his clinician and
a man to see to his wishes. I regret that our
respective jobs in this have put us in conflict.
But as I told you it is nothing personal. Of
that I can assure you.
I wish you the best with your writing.

Regards,

Marko Novak.

Part III

From the heart of a murderer

… SHE LAY LIMP ON the mattress, the bedclothes halfway up her back. One hand stretched out ahead of her, palm down. Her hair fell over her shoulder and partly across her face. She looked almost sultry, he thought, and imagined she was striking this pose for him; elongated and sensual as a cat. But this abstraction was interrupted by a thick crimson ichor oozing from beneath her hairline and congealing in a sticky-looking black mud. Then a more dilute trickle seeped from the clump of blood and hair and pooled in the concave at her temple.

He reached into the top drawer of the bedside locker, bunched some underwear in his fist and dabbed at the blood. It soaked through and he left it pressed against her temple.

Sucking from the depths, he found no breath in his lungs. An invisible wound had perforated his chest, like a burrowing wormhole. Stooped over her, unable to save or forsake, a tear was drawn by the irrevocable. He was precariously perched between two worlds, and to his surprise had become ineffectual in both. The memory of her petrified stare, a floating, ethereal thing, locked down on him. A crosscurrent shifting and pulling him through a fog of cognisance. 'You have never been a victim,' he said. 'Wouldn't allow yourself to be. And neither will I.'

Straightening himself, he looked about the room. Then he pulled the tarpaulin over alongside the bed and spread it out. He tried to turn her onto her back so that he could sweep her up—draping her body across his arms in one last throe of distorted sentimentality—and lay her gently down. But she had fallen too close to the edge of the bed and she rolled, her torso tumbling toward him. His arms shot outward and caught her before she hit the floor. For a few awkward moments he was able to hold her steady. Then, as he set himself to lift the body back onto the bed, so that he might start again, her hips and legs slunk off the bed too, flopping and slipping and causing the whole weight of her to come down on top of him. It brought him to his knees, on the floor, as she dropped leaden in front of him. She lay inert, her neck and head thrown backward over his forearm. Her eyes were opened and seemed to stare at something just above the skirting board on the other side of the room. He slipped his arm out from under her, apologising all the way, and rolled her up into the tarpaulin sheet; there was no stopping now. Not to think; not to feel; not to regret.

'It's a burdensome quest I am entrusted with here, Val. A job that has to be done.' Valerie, now just a weight in an industrial blanket, was easier to consider. Easier to talk to. 'Other men wouldn't have the stomach for it. Nor the vision. We are victims, of course we are, but it is naïve to think that victims aren't necessary elements of human life.'

He had tied the tarpaulin tightly and sat panting and dripping with sweat on the side of the bed. A bead of perspiration slid from his forehead, down his nose and splashed on the blue sheet below. Another bead dropped but he caught it in his palm and then watched as two more dropped on top of it.

'It isn't that I don't love you, Val. You should know that. For I do. In many respects you are the essence of my life. My whole body cries for you. See,' he said, holding aloft his sweaty palm. But know this, my love, though my eyes must now be stoic, my body will know who you have been. Who you are … Duty: that god-awful burden. And mine is as awful as any man has ever borne.'

Wiping his brow then, he sat listening, his wife dead at his feet, and tried to remember why it had to be so.

'For Aimeé Quinn,' he muttered.

Then said it again, and again, as if by way of repetition better sense might be made of it. He worked to recall Aimeé Quinn but failed. Each time the flittering light of the TV lifted the shadow from the rolled up package on the floor he lost the precious vision of Aimeé Quinn. There was only an intuited feeling of exaggeration about her.

Eventually, he stopped sweating and stood up. He took hold of the tarpaulin, at the end where Valerie's feet were, and began to drag her toward the landing. The tarpaulin was new and clean, and it slid easily across the carpet. At the stairs he thought of Vinny Bolzano, the kid dragged down the stairs by his own family, his head bouncing like a coconut all the way. A rat, he was. 'You're no rat though, are you, Val?'

No, she was something beautiful. Something floral. Like a lilac or freesia, he thought. Symbolic; purity and cheer, faithfulness and sweetness... simplicity.

Hunched, breathless, hands on hips, this was what occurred to him. What he loved most was Valerie's simplicity. No matter how ridiculous or forthright or gushing or naked, her thoughts and feelings were always verbalised, and they were unabashed. That trueness was something he could admire, even now, so late in the final act.

He felt the urge to look at her face then—one last time—but baulked at the idea of unwrapping her. Then another image wandered in and he thought he might prop her up at the kitchen table, and the two of them could sit down with a cup of tea. He could talk with her... to her... but the wormhole in his chest opened up again, boring deeper into him. His eyes cried.

But quickly he shut the door on these thoughts and manoeuvred her upright against the banisters, on the landing. Crouching down, he allowed her to fall over his shoulder. Heaving and lifting, he had her up, balancing and testing the weight of her like a log-bearing lumberjack. The rasping whisper of tarpaulin, creasing and rippling, allowed him to imagine something not as onerous upon his shoulder.

At the bottom of the stairs, aware that their exit needed to be swift, he swivelled her into a chair in the hallway, so that he could have the boot opened and the way clear. As he looked at her in the chair, motionless behind her strange blue burqa, he was unsure whether he'd sat her down the wrong way up.

'Though you might prefer that,' he said.

When they had first lived together, he had come home to the peculiar sight of Valerie with her legs just thrown over the back of the sofa. Hanging upside down. Her shoulders, neck, and head would slump over the edge, dangling like a dead weight. She'd just make a decision and throw her feet over her head at any moment it occurred to her. The rush of blood downwards, the lightness in the legs against the heaviness of the head, soothed, she said. 'Like being in a safe kind of free fall, Al. You should try it!' she'd call out to him, as if she was riding a rollercoaster, having the time of her life.

He would try to read a book on another seat, or pretend he was reading, while she hung there and watched TV. He couldn't understand her. 'Based on no theory or teaching,' he once told her, 'you have discovered that the physical sensation achieved by dangling upside down satisfies something in you, and you simply indulge it. Without hesitation! It's interesting to me, this capacity of yours. I admire it. Love it even.'

She liked it so she did it. This was what he meant by simplicity. This was what he fell in love with. 'It's quite marvellous actually, Val. I'm in awe of you,' he told her.

Her certainty of self was not an intelligent thing, though, he also told her, years later; when she had become less extraordinary to him and the first thoughts of wanting to be without her manifested. His desire for solitude was strictly emotional, psychological, at that stage.

He had grown disappointed in life, in himself, and regretted how passively he had lived. He had come to envy Valerie's fearlessness. But unable to admit that, he began to resent her. Secretly. He constructed a story of a man at the end of his tether, a man who could no longer be held back by the stupidity of his wife. 'There is though,' he told her, as a means of tempering the cruelty, 'something of the profound in that certainty of yours. Something universal yet elusive lies within it. A truth, if there is such a thing. For you are happier than me.'

Many of Valerie's actions, habits and thoughts were absurd, or eccentric to him. But beautifully so. You could not convey what was wonderful in Valerie through words. You had to see her. Be with her. Then you could make sense of the incongruity. The neat appearance, clean and formally attractive, and the distinct quirkiness of soul. It was really something to see her behind closed doors, where the intimacy of her little madnesses were observable in the flesh. To witness the ease with which she made her reasons reasonable. It was irresistible.

Remembering her and seeing her before him, swathed in a blue plastic blanket, was uncomfortable. He was saddened. Remembering them as a couple, in their respective primes, and the hopes he had of them aging gracefully. There had been magic in their aesthetic, although he was a little embarrassed by the superficiality that underpinned his affection for her. She had never been embarrassed by it, which seemed now, to him, an entirely honest way to meet life and love; acknowledging the flesh and deception of it.

He had been telling himself for many years that it was Valerie who changed, not him. The physical change was inevitable, even he accepted that, however repulsed he had become by the folds, wrinkles, discolouration and rottings of life. But he now realised that in a way - in a crucial way—Valerie had never changed. She had been as irrepressibly herself an hour before as she had been that first time he found her hanging upside down on the sofa, them having known each other barely three months. It was him, Albert Jackson, who had changed. He'd never been himself in the first place, perhaps.

'Who am I then?' he asked.

And what a time to be asking, he thought.

Who am I? he wondered. What have I become? When did the boy become the man, and the man become a different kind of man? How many different men have I been? To my parents, my siblings, my friends, my colleagues, my students and my very own sweet children?

His sweet children! 'Jake and Abi.'

Jake had been an experience unlike any Albert had ever known. Even now, when Albert looked at Jake - in his adult-hood, as opinionated and stubborn as Albert had ever been—he could be taken back years. To when he loved Jake with a tender-ness so immense that it defied cynicism. Jake, as the first born will, tutored Albert in aspects of life that may as well not have existed before. For all Albert had known of them.

He had always known that his children, when eventually they arrived, would be loved, and that he'd step up and provide, but he overlooked the possibility that *they* could affect *him*. When Jake was only a newborn, on a weekend or during holidays, Albert often took him to the master bedroom, drew the curtains and lay down on the bed, to allow Jake to take his mid-morning nap with him. Though it may have happened only a handful of times, and each time differently, Albert remembered the scene as if all occasions of Jake falling asleep on him had been one: the bedroom draped in whispers and cooing; streams of morning sun pulsating through the gold, polyester curtains and drenching the room in an atmospheric ecru glow; particles dancing in and out of the beams; the boys soft head jigsawed between Albert's jaw and clavicle; his moth breath on Albert's bare chest; the lanugo feel of the boy's back as Albert stroked it in circles and rested his stubbly chin on his fluffy head. The peace. The oneness. The tiny vulnerability of the child against its towering power to evoke. The pure devotion; Albert had not expected it.

By the time Abi had been born no such peace existed; it had been the special privilege of the first born. Albert was only ever able to remember Abi with Jake milling about her, sharing or demanding attention at turns. No, the bond with the daughter had been formed in different ways.

'What kind of father will they remember?' he wondered. And would that father bear any relation to any of the men he remembered himself as being?

And Valerie too? How many Alberts had she known? And how compromised were they now, having seen what she saw with her last glance? He thought that the man he presented to Valerie on that very first night at the bar twenty-five-plus years before had been a fraud; his best impersonation of the man he wished he would one day become. He dressed and talked like that man, turning his shoulder to the world in the manner he expected such a man would do, but who was he really? Albert grew into the world-weary character he thought would impress others. But looking back, he wasn't sure he had ever been that man;

indifferent, cocksure, worldly, cultured, cynical, savvy. What he was, really, in his heart, was an idealist. A dreamer. A hoper.

Albert had been a gentle boy, wary of conflict and sensitive to the pain of others. But he buried that boy somewhere along the way. And although that boy still kicked at the box in his shallow grave, he had been well and truly buried; buried alive, unknown even to Albert, until now. 'And when I found out about that boy, Val, when I realised how I'd wasted my life holding back and judging and being afraid to be seen trying, I blamed you.' Blamed Valerie, sweet Valerie, who had loved him and known him and brought the only joys he'd known in his life; his life, that farcical performance! He'd wasted it pretending he had no interest in it.

'Val, I'm so sorry,' he said, struggling with her to the front door, bleeding tears all over her blue funeral suit.

It was past midnight and there was hardly cause to expect passersby or even watchers from neighbouring windows. The evening was still and mild. The moon was a pear, not quite full but bright in the blue-black sky.

He had opened the boot of the Estate in preparation but had not thought to turn the car around and save himself ten yards and considerable exposure. Too late to turn back with the body—she was already up in his arms—he proceeded as quickly as possible. He angled her toward the front door with precision, with a hardened poise, only for the sight of a tube of Russian-red lipstick on the hall table to open up that wormhole to his heart again. His knees buckled. She crashed from his arms and he after her. With a kneading ache through his chest, he dragged her out the door and down the front path to the car.

'Alright, Sir? Need a hand?'

Who the fuck! he thought, and spun around.

Valerie's wrapped body was lying on the ground to the rear of the car. Albert was breathing heavily, trying to be clear and calculating while at the same time trying not to think at all. He put his hand to his chest and reared back, wincing.

'You need a hand?'

'What're you doing here?'

'Oh … eh … nothing. On my way home. Stopped for a little lie down. Lovely bit of lawn you have there, Sir. Lookin' at the stars there. Nearly asleep. When the light came out the door and frightened the shit out of me.'

Albert glared at the boy. And the boy apologised wordlessly. Head down. Quiet. Sure that it was the swearing that had caused the offense.

'Move along, Atley. Go home. School in the morning.'

'Sure you don't need a hand?'

'No. Go home.'

But Simon Atley continued across Albert's lawn, walking straight over the rose bed. 'For Christ's sake, Atley!'

'Oh, fuck! Sorry, Sir. Didn't notice. Honest,' he said, trying to reverse out of the bed but stumbling over his sea legs and ending up sprawled out with his nose to the rolled tarpaulin on the ground. 'Seriously, sorry about that,' he said, getting up. 'Just wasn't looking where I was going. Rough night and all. Look, let me give you a hand here,' he said, and before Albert could stop him he was helping work the tarpaulin package so that it was standing against the bumper. Then the boy went to lift it from the feet, and tip it fully into the boot. But as Atley went to lift the feet, Albert moved across him.

'That'll do fine, thanks.' He shoved Atley away, then quickly turned and rolled the body fully into the boot himself. When he looked back around, Atley had sobered up, miraculously. He was nodding manically, backing away from Albert, pointing over his shoulder with his thumb.

'I'll be off then, Sir.'

Albert took a long look at Atley before closing up the boot and getting into the car. He reversed at high speed as Atley watched from the end of the driveway. The front door of the house remained open and Albert took a mental snapshot of it, knowing what it might mean to somebody else, before speeding off towards the sea …

As a young couple, all that while ago, the sea had been the place closest to their hearts. The sound and the smell of the coast were fixed within them. Sometimes when they drove along the coast road, on a warm night, with the windows rolled down, the sea-weedy, salty, pungent freshness of it filled the car and made Albert nostalgic for some indistinct childhood experience. As a matter of habit, he checked the tides in the paper, daily, noting highs and lows. He regularly took his exercise on a route past the sea too, when the weather was close and muggy and he knew where the tide would be. That smell of the sea, that smell of summer and home, he was always seeking. The sea to him was a memory devoid of imagery or occasion. It was just a feeling. A need.

It was also where Valerie told him she was pregnant with Abigail. An August evening following a blistering day of sunshine. There were only a scattering of people left on the beach when they arrived and the sun was falling fast onto the choppy blackness of the low hills behind. Jake was with Albert, two, maybe three years old then, sitting between Albert's bent legs on the sand. Shivering. In a towel. Albert warmed him with his hands, rubbing him briskly about the upper arms. They were close to the water and waiting as Valerie took her turn to swim. She came out of the water looking bronzed, her skin pimpled and tight from the cold water. Her long hair was scooped over one shoulder and the whites of her eyes were alight as she looked to her boys. Then her hand moved unconsciously across her belly.

Albert looked from her hand to her face and knew. She smiled. He leapt onto his feet and had her in his arms before she ever got the words out. Then he lifted Jake up into his arms and they all stood warming each other in a circled embrace. As the sand grew dark and the sea crashed rhythmically in the background, they gathered their towels and walked hand in hand into the setting sun, towards the car and home.

'So, to the sea,' he said.

It was a ten minute drive ordinarily but that night, having initially sped away from the house and Simon Atley, Albert drove cautiously. He didn't want to draw attention. 'If I can get us to the sea we might be alright, Val,' he spoke over his shoulder, as she lay mum in the boot.

The back roads were narrow and high-walled. Even in

daylight, shadows were cast over them by the billowing branches of trees overhead. An occasional street lamp, dimmed by coatings of dead flies and microscopic tendrils and specks of dirt and grime inside their casing, provided some light. But it was mostly the clear sky and the pear-shaped moon that lit the way.

Albert knew the road well and he coasted detachedly through the earliest hours. The smooth swerve around familiar bends, the subtle acceleration into stretches of known good road, and the soft break of the car as he approached blind spots, lulled his mind to near restfulness. He had forgotten how much he enjoyed driving. 'This is why the automobile continues to prevail,' he told her, 'even knowing all that we know about greenhouse gases, carbon footprints, and finite resources. Autonomy, freedom, escape.'

She said nothing back.

'Escape,' he said again.

This was not what he had in mind, though. He would never escape, he knew.

'My entire history, everything I am, whatever posterity will judge that to be, is here, Val. My home. Our home. We'll not leave,' he promised her.

His *story*, all his worthwhile experiences were embedded in the roads, the sands, the pavements, the buildings, the classrooms, the faces of the place; the town and its surrounding wildernesses were alive with the tacit knowledge of a given place that all men retain somewhere within themselves, and at some time will feel nostalgic for.

'For me, that place is here, Val. Right here before us, and around us. You know, I once read—can't remember where— 'Home is not a place but an accumulation of experience.' And I believe that. I really do. I feel like I've been reaching out to touch that experience all my life. That my frustrations are because I haven't been able to. But now I'm starting to understand that we're not supposed to touch it, to really get at it. Isn't that accumulation of experience what makes it all magic? What ensures our uniqueness. I believe that life is this accumulation, Val. That's what I believe.' He chased the back roads further into the night

as he listened to her silence and heard it as if it were affirma-
tion. 'This place is our home. I'll not leave it now. I'll not leave
you. Though it gives me wings, I have no need of them,' he
said, laughing at the unmistakably bogus rhetoric that inevitably
slipped into such conversation; articulation of the celestial can
only ever end in laughable failure.

He thought to cry again but did not.

Before long, he turned and eased the car to a stop at a layby,
where, through a break in an old stone wall, you could pass onto
a track through the sparse dunes, down to the shore. Turning
off the engine and sitting a while in the silence, the night sky
above the sea line panned out before them. 'Remember, Val?
Remember the night. I was thinking of it, only just now. You
were never so beautiful as that night. How the moon spilled over
your face. Life inside you. And how you smiled. One of those
real smiles, the whole night long.'

In fact, he remembered, she had smiled in her sleep. He'd
watched her fall asleep and woken up ahead of her. She was still
smiling. The happiest of times.

He waited to make sure the way was clear before getting
out of the car. The deep clunk of the closing door sounded out
against the night. Over the broken wall and the low dunes, he
could hear the sea whispering onto the sand and smell it on the
breeze. Then he lifted his head and looked out toward the sea
again to see the moon splashing its silver and the ripples shimmering in the distance. 'It is surely sights such as this that make
men dream of gods. And of conquering foreign lands, and set
them to wondering at the miracle of life,' he sighed.

At the boot, he searched for his breath again, appreciating
that haste was imperative, and set to work. He tried to lift the
body but couldn't and was forced to drag it, breathlessly and
haphazardly, from the boot onto the ground; her body falling
like a deck of cards, limbs floating, strewn at random. Her bare
feet now protruded clearly from one end and he worked his
hands in under the loosened wrapping and grabbed her ankles.
He turned her twice, rolling her tightly back into the tarpaulin
and knotted the rope again.

By the time he got her the short distance to the wall he was exhausted. The tarpaulin had frayed in places. He paused, wearied by the relentless gravity of what he'd done, and wondered how to get her over the rocky rubble of the collapsed wall, and down the small drop behind without... hurting her...

But then, from along the road he had driven, he heard voices. In rising panic he fell to his knees. With his fingers, first, then his hands and forearms, he got in under her weight and managed to lift her about a foot above the ground. Then he half rolled and half pushed her body through the break in the wall. But she folded at what he guessed was about a one-hundred and sixty-degree angle, and became jammed in the gap, ass out to sea.

The voices rounded the trees on one end of the layby and he drew back his foot, knee to midriff, and stomped down and outward, into what must have been her hip and stomach, sending her thudding down behind the wall and hitting the fine sand with a deadness that chilled.

'I'm just saying that I love you. I know it won't change. It doesn't matter if...' a young man keened.

'And I love you—you know that!' the woman responded.

He listened quietly, standing still, hoping they wouldn't notice him. But he could hear their footsteps grow slow and knew he'd have to turn around. Sucking back the barely supressed emotions, he turned to face them.

'Good evening,' they said in unison.

'Fine mild night, alright,' he responded, smiling as best he could.

'Yeah, fantastic for this time of year,' the young man said.

They continued walking and he waved them languidly onwards, watching their shadowy figures moving away through the night. He considered their greying silhouette—an emblem of young love: hand in hand; two pairs of drain-piped legs and comfortable trainers; the young man's hood bunched about his shoulders; her hair dancing in a ponytail behind her; and the enduring impression of the young man as a man like any other on the precipice of life, standing tall and slim and confident, sure of the future, gesturing to the moon in emphasis of his heartfelt point.

'They were us once, Val,' Albert whispered over the wall and onto the sand. 'Walking these roads, in sweet disagreement over the meaning of our love for each other.' These discussions always ended in an inevitable but loving embrace; no agreement reached, but apprehension having been coaxed into retreat...

For Albert there had been three phases in their marriage. The first was a continuation of what he had just observed, a time when all was well—intense, intimate, unsettling at times, but essentially good. The times we look back upon in later life and remember most fondly because they are most vital. From their earliest courtship into the first few years of marriage, this had been life for Albert and Valerie. They both worked, came home and dined together. They took long walks in the summer evenings and during winter Valerie would pass the night watching TV, gossiping on the phone or under the guise of a Residents Association meeting, while he read or exercised or prepared work for the following day. *Balance* was the word that best defined this period of his life. He felt healthy of mind and body. He was still drawn to her company and her beauty, and they seemed to exist in symbiosis.

He couldn't remember the day or month, or even a season or year, but he recalled the occasion where the concept of *imbalance* tottered across the living room. It was a midterm, or perhaps Christmas or Easter break. He'd begun writing poetry and dabbling in short stories, and had taken to sitting in the living room at night, looking wistfully at the lined notepad on his leg, pen in hand, summoning ideas, phrases, clauses, sentences and working on them like a mitt, until they took recognizable form and began to shine. He fancied himself quite the preeminent aesthete then, in his chair, one leg across the other. He took immense enjoyment from the notion he had of Valerie as his doting muse, waiting night after night for the wonder he would one day produce and she would be the first to set eyes upon. Then one evening, middle of the week or thereabouts, he heard the distinctive rhythm of purpose crossing the kitchen tiles and then onto the wood of the living room. The sleek percussion of her stride swished and swivelled to a stop in the middle of the room. She looked devastating; the embodiment of the woman he had married and coveted, the woman he had wanted all his life, from before he even knew he wanted such things.

'Al, the R.A. guys are coming over, remember? We're going to need to set the table and organise these two rooms a bit. And I'm going to need you to do drinks, okay?'

She was dressed as she always dressed when she was intent on something, in a hugging skirt, falling just below the knee, with a slightly billowing blouse tucked into the high waist. That night, the skirt had a racy thigh split and the blouse was sleeveless, buttoned and cream. The outline of her body was discreetly present wherever he looked—her waist, her still firm stomach, her swelling breasts. Makeup was executed to fine precision, her eyes shining and her face effortlessly suspended in the delicate mould of her hair. She ran her hands down the side of her skirt and back up the contours of her backside as she looked at herself in the mirror over the fireplace; he noticed nails, painted a slightly darker shade of lavender than he might have expected. For the first time since they'd known each other, it occurred to him, 'This isn't for me.' The elaborate ritual of primping and preening that was a precursor for any occasion had always kept one eye on him and indulged his tastes. For the first time he was aware of, Valerie had no interest in what he thought she looked like. She was out to knock other people dead. And it followed, then, that if he had been shifted from the centre of her intimate universe, then so had his vain ideas about himself.

'Sure, Val,' he said, and never again wrote so much as a shopping list in her presence.

Albert's fantasy, the myth of self that had been gestating in his mind all his life—the arrogant adolescent dreams of undefined greatness, the inferred conceitedness of his attack on his parents' simple values and the resultant stonewalling of his siblings for fear of contagion, the ostentatious role assumed in the early years of marriage—was infiltrated by reality. His wife reached out into the wider world, looking for another definition of self, one that was amputated of Albert's influence, and it killed him;

the disappointment of the future was no longer deniable.

The second phase of their marriage was a period during which these realisations crystalised, beginning in that moment, lasting almost the entirety of the marriage, and ending as he entered the fatal third phase. During these arduous years, Albert carried his silent rejection everywhere. With each party, occasion, community meeting that Valerie arranged, prepared for and attended, he sank further into himself. He sulked so long and with such conviction that the narrative of Albert's legendary aloofness became, even to Valerie, engrained as truth: it was just Al; always been this way; doesn't mean any offence; don't read anything into it; that's just Albert being Albert. He never spoke of that evening of the Residents Association meeting to Valerie, never confessed his dreams or fears.

The fact that something in him had been irredeemably corrupted became less obvious the more accustomed he became to playing at social ineptitude. He settled into the strangeness of his assumed role, immune to Valerie's embarrassment or annoyance. Seemingly content, he dreamt up new ways to resent Valerie: hating her for her inability to exist in silence; the way she asked for the salt or asked him how many sugars he put in her coffee— almost accusatory in tone; or ran her tongue over her front teeth after applying lipstick; or bought glossy magazines and left them unread on the coffee table for weeks and then threw them out. Even the things that should have pleased him began to irritate him. He hated the way she folded towels, the way she stacked the dishwasher, the way she filed his bills and receipts for him. The manner of everything she did came to seem illogical and deliberately seditious.

The point of transition to the third phase was less easy to locate. What he could say was that the third phase had been passed into comparatively recently and once entered into, it moved apace; at least as swiftly as glorious youth viewed through the eyes of an ancient man. He could tell himself that he loved her, and felt certain that it was true, but he couldn't feel it. Impending doom was written in the stars.

Then came Aimeé Quinn. The raw youth of her. Sweetness.

He just found himself peering across the staffroom at her, or down long corridors, and wondering. Just as he had found each tiny nuance of Valerie's manner and outlook offensive, he began to see innocence and purity in Aimeé's : in the new top she wore; the way her hair was tied back, or up, or was braided or plaited; her personalised coffee mug—Quinn-t-essential !; her new car; the pleasant jocosity of her; the tilt of her head, the lilt of her voice; the dramas, the novels, the poets she chose to teach; and the books she read (though he never would have read such things himself). They all spoke to him of her sweetness, and decency. Aimeé began life in Albert's world as a pleasant distraction from the failure and disappointment of life.

He wanted to get near to her but was never so crude as to engineer a meeting, or an opportunity to sit near her at lunch. But on occasion it would happen organically—she would be last in, having spent ten minutes goading or coaxing some imbecile into doing their homework for the following day, and there would be only one seat left. Beside Albert.

They talked. It was easy. Comfortable. The next time they'd talk again. She seemed interested in him, looking in his eyes as he spoke, smiling kindly. On one occasion she touched his arm as she laughed guiltily at one of his acrid observations. He felt bigger in her presence. He began to love her, or some idea of her, and grew jealous of other people's interactions with her.

Nicholas Jones was the proverbial straw. Albert perceived Nicholas Jones' pursuit of her and envisaged, for the second time in his life, his dreams slipping away. And he was not prepared to live without them ...

The sand where Valerie's body fell was so fine that he could achieve no secure footing. He had to drag and pull and heave, moving her only a bare few yards at a time. Forced to use all his weight, leaning back until he fell over, standing and going at it again, they struggled through the sand. As they snaked through the dunes the fineness of the sand was quick to fill the shallow trench they furrowed; tiny grains, unable to hold, pouring in and covering over the track left by the dragging feet. The breeze whispered through the arrow grass and sea daisies scattered about on the dunes and the timeless sea crept nearer, as if rising to meet them.

Eventually he dragged her from between two egg-shaped dunes, within sight of the water. He untied the rope, rolled her gently out and let the tarpaulin loose. The plastic sheet stood up for a moment on the breeze, creased and wavering, before tumbling rigidly away to the side and getting caught on a dune where the arrow grass grew thickest.

Out on the exposed beach, the night was brighter again and he could see more clearly. Her face was rigid and gaunt, so unalive that he couldn't bear to look. Without life, Valerie was not Valerie. He twisted tiredly from his knees to a sitting position, unable to consider her as she lay. Sat beside her, looking out across the night with her laid out beside him like some hopelessly devout moonbather, desperately drinking in all the lunar possibility in the milky night. He began again to talk with her.

'It makes me sick to think of it now. How I looked upon that girl, Val. I never meant to betray you. I swear. I realise now... realise what we've got. Can you ever forgive me?'

In the silence that followed he wept loudly and with abandon.

After some minutes he brought the sobbing under control. 'It'll take time. I recognise that. But I want you to know... I know you do... somewhere in your heart. I want you to hear me, want to tell you—I love you, Val.' Those words had been absent too long or used so reflexively that they had lost their impact. Lost the unspeakable depth of when first they were spoken. 'Do you remember? How it stuttered out of me. I had wanted it to be a declaration. Something strong and dependable. Something unsentimental, in fact. Can you imagine? Unsentimental! What an ass I've been, Val. What is love if not sentimental? And for all my ideas of how I would declare it, for how I wanted you to see me as I told you, it simply fell out in the end. Exactly the thing I didn't want it to be; a heap of nerves and uncertainty. All that's good in love, ironically. The high-wire vulnerability! Of telling somebody that first time. That's what it's all about, isn't it? Of course, you'd shown your hand already, by the time I... but all the same... you can't exist solely in a cocoon, can you? Not your whole life. You've got to believe in something.'

And he had betrayed it.

He brushed the last traces of those tears from his eyes with his shirt sleeve. Then, cradling the back of her head in one palm, he scooped some sand in behind her neck, to support her head and make her comfortable. It was time.

The sea was floating at eye-level. In wait of them.

He left her lying in the looming dunes, cold on the cold sand, head propped up and the drawn colour of her mortality softened by the light of those nocturnal liars—the stars, the moon, the darkness. Several minutes later, his feet could be heard swivelling and squeezing through the sand underfoot, returning from his car with only the glinting shovel; he had left the saw in the boot, and was glad of it. The thought of it now seemed unbearably violent. It was part of another time. A different him. A different idea about how things would end. There was a new conclusion now.

Arriving back where she lay, he did not stop to talk or look down. Instead he walked straight on, down close to the sea, and spiked the wet sand with the shovel. The sound of the water was soft and rhythmic.

'What's done is done,' he said.

Valerie's body had assumed greater weight—the gravity of death leaning an elbow on the scales—and she seemed to be spilling disobediently from his arms. His legs were weakening ever further and he stumbled onto the sand several times. Each time he rose from his knees with her in his arms, he imagined himself a noble warrior, trudging through the mire to recover the body of his lover; walking ten thousand miles or more, just to bring her home. 'The sea awaits us, my love,' he said, but her blank stare wouldn't look to him.

At the water's edge he lay her down on the sloping sand, feet brushed by the foamy water of hard breaking waves. He took off his trainers and socks, rolled his trousers up to his knees and dug into the sand beside her.

Soon he had a hole, a couple of feet deep and half the length of her body. He was exhausted and the tide was coming in too fast. He couldn't dig quickly enough and was no longer sure why he was digging at all. A grave? To hide her? That was not why they were here. 'I'm confused now, Val,' he admitted, sitting down beside her. 'I don't know how to bring you back.'

On the horizon he detected night's dark pall giving way to the dawn. The tide was rising and a wakeless impulse for ceremony yenned within him. He sat into the hole he had dug and reached out for her. It took all his remaining strength to take hold of her and pull her across the sand, and then down on top of him. He opened his thighs as wide as the hole allowed and propped her between them, lying her back against his chest. Her cold head and matted hair slumped against his right shoulder, slightly turned, and he fed his arms in under hers and locked his hands tightly together across her middle; a final pyrrhic embrace. 'We will wait. Let the sea come for us. We are ready now. Let it come. We've nothing to be sorry for, my love,' he whispered in her ear.

He cried down one side of her face. The tears rolled into the neckline of her pyjamas and he imagined them soaking through her breastbone and penetrating her heart; and he saw her heart healing, heard it hearing his aching lament. His profound regret.

They sat locked together more intimately than they ever had in life and he believed that his sorrow had reached her soul. They watched the sky diffuse to a rich blue, and the low-builded cloud disperse as the sun's surreal crown rose from beyond the horizon. The sea seemed even more gentle in the early light and he was overcome by a sudden need to tell her everything about himself, to share with her all the tiny moments of his life, moments that must have been somehow instrumental in forging him because they were all he could really remember now. 'I only know that, even as a boy, I think maybe six or seven, or whenever self-awareness began, I suffered an untreatable feeling of loneliness. I didn't lack company. I had a loving family, as you know. In the end it was I who rejected them. And I had friends back then. It was not for lack of company that I felt it. There was just an immense vacuity in me, something that neither kin nor friend could fill. As I got older and expressed versions of this story, my parents attempted to persuade me that what was missing was God. Faith. But it wasn't. Or maybe it was but I didn't have the capacity for that kind of collective delusion. I just felt empty. Didn't know what to do with death. Didn't know why a life was worth living if it wasn't significant. And even at that, didn't know if significance was all that significant in the end. The point of life seemed to be to enjoy it while it lasted. Which was fine but all the aspects of life people categorised as enjoyable seemed to me to be ways of avoiding the inevitable. So what's the point? That's where it all began. Disappointment has defined my life. From the beginning.'

Soon after, morning broke with definitiveness. In that early haze they were still just two silhouetted lovers, legless on the strand, gazing out to sea, in awe of the brand-new dawn, of love, of themselves. He continued to talk to her for as long as he could believe she was listening. 'And now I have become the thing I most revile—a disappointment. Do you remember what I was when we first met, Val? Do you? Because I've no idea anymore. Don't even know what I wanted to be back then. What did you see? And how did I end up here? I'm so sorry. Sorrier than I'll ever be able to express. One dreams, at the very least, of redeeming one's self in the end. But there's no way that can be true now, is there? What must you have thought? I'm haunted by it. They won't understand, Val. How could they? They won't understand,' he said again, crying again on her shoulder. 'I didn't mean it. You know that, don't you? You know that.'

The sea had swallowed their legs and hips. The sand now mudded on their thighs, a silty spread, burying them deeper in the hole he had dug for them with each rush of water up the beach. He kissed her hair and left his lips resting on her head. The tributary of words ran dry and finally there were no more tears; for there couldn't be.

He had no sense of what was amassing behind him, in virtual silence. The first he knew of it was when he felt a hand at his back, 'Excuse me, are you okay? Can you tell us your name?'

He couldn't, for he didn't know who he was anymore.

A second man bent down in front of Valerie. He had inclined his head and was speaking gently to her. He put his middle and index finger to her neck, just below the curve of her jaw, and looked solemn but said nothing. The two men looked at each other and then followed Albert's gaze out to sea, and somehow, for some reason, it was only then he observed their uniforms.

He didn't notice either of them calling for assistance or the arrival of others, but soon heard the whispering around him, observed people coming into earshot and retreating back out to discuss or explain or instruct. Another man came before him and looked him in the eye. 'We need to take her now, sir. Okay? We need you to release your hands.' The officer had taken Albert's wrists as he spoke and gently lifted his interlocked hands to the side. Albert noted the strange warmth of the officer's touch and its absence when he let go.

Then began his awareness of several other bodies about him, moving around, sizing the situation up. He felt Valerie's weight leaving his thighs, his torso, and he felt an instantaneous loneliness. The cool breeze gusted about him. 'Now you,' another voice said, this one harder, less patient. 'On your feet.'

'Cuffs?' somebody asked.

Albert's hands extended willingly, as if in surrender to something he had not yet fully acknowledged.

'No,' the hard voice responded.

Taking a last look at the sea, their sea, he turned to walk up the beach. His mind floated free of the scene and he could feel his body no longer, gliding along, partly on his feet and partly swept along by the hands clasped at his elbows.

A small crowd had gathered but he paid it little heed. No face stuck out as either familiar or notable. On his left shoulder he heard one of the officers say, 'Move him along. Quick as we can.'

Whatever it was the officer feared, Albert sensed none of it. He was aware of being looked at, followed by so many eyes and wondered after, but still no familiar voice came from the watchers.

In the layby there were a handful of vehicles—his own and several police cars and an ambulance. He was led through the break in the wall and towards the open door of a police car. An officer held the door open and showed Albert onto the backseat before shutting it. His window was closed and he sat alone on the backseat, all the emotions of the night suddenly closed off. The car was warm and he felt sleepy.

He could still hear the conversation around the car, as if listening through a cup and string, even as his head began to nod onto his chest and the heaviness of his eyelids grew more insistent.

'What's happened?' he heard someone ask.

There were so many voices that he couldn't follow which was which. There was only one that stood out, the hard voice making the decisions. But it had no face to go with it. The only face available to him was Valerie's; ashen, horrified, bloodied.

And then the hard voice again.

'Looks like the crazy fucker killed his wife,' it said I'd killed my Val.

JOHN TOOMEY was born in 1975 in Dublin, where he now teaches English at Clonkeen College. He is the author of *Sleepwalker* and *Huddleston Road*, both of which are available from Dalkey Archive Press.

MICHAL AJVAZ, *The Golden Age.*
The Other City.
PIERRE ALBERT-BIROT, *Grabinoulor.*
YUZ ALESHKOVSKY, *Kangaroo.*
FELIPE ALFAU, *Chromos.*
Locos.
JOE AMATO, *Samuel Taylor's Last Night.*
IVAN ÂNGELO, *The Celebration.*
The Tower of Glass.
ANTÓNIO LOBO ANTUNES, *Knowledge of Hell.*
The Splendor of Portugal.
ALAIN ARIAS-MISSON, *Theatre of Incest.*
JOHN ASHBERY & JAMES SCHUYLER, *A Nest of Ninnies.*
ROBERT ASHLEY, *Perfect Lives.*
GABRIELA AVIGUR-ROTEM, *Heatwave and Crazy Birds.*
DJUNA BARNES, *Ladies Almanack.*
Ryder.
JOHN BARTH, *Letters.*
Sabbatical.
DONALD BARTHELME, *The King.*
Paradise.
SVETISLAV BASARA, *Chinese Letter.*
MIQUEL BAUÇÀ, *The Siege in the Room.*
RENÉ BELLETTO, *Dying.*
MAREK BIENCZYK, *Transparency.*
ANDREI BITOV, *Pushkin House.*
ANDREJ BLATNIK, *You Do Understand.*
Law of Desire.
LOUIS PAUL BOON, *Chapel Road.*
My Little War.
Summer in Termuren.
ROGER BOYLAN, *Killoyle.*
IGNÁCIO DE LOYOLA BRANDÃO, *Anonymous Celebrity.*
Zero.
BONNIE BREMSER, *Troia: Mexican Memoirs.*
CHRISTINE BROOKE-ROSE, *Amalgamemnon.*
BRIGID BROPHY, *In Transit.*
The Prancing Novelist.

GERALD L. BRUNS, *Modern Poetry and the Idea of Language.*
GABRIELLE BURTON, *Heartbreak Hotel.*
MICHEL BUTOR, *Degrees.*
Mobile.
G. CABRERA INFANTE, *Infante's Inferno.*
Three Trapped Tigers.
JULIETA CAMPOS, *The Fear of Losing Eurydice.*
ANNE CARSON, *Eros the Bittersweet.*
ORLY CASTEL-BLOOM, *Dolly City.*
LOUIS-FERDINAND CÉLINE, *North.*
Conversations with Professor Y.
London Bridge.
MARIE CHAIX, *The Laurels of Lake Constance.*
HUGO CHARTERIS, *The Tide Is Right.*
ERIC CHEVILLARD, *Demolishing Nisard.*
The Author and Me.
MARC CHOLODENKO, *Mordechai Schamz.*
JOSHUA COHEN, *Witz.*
EMILY HOLMES COLEMAN, *The Shutter of Snow.*
ERIC CHEVILLARD, *The Author and Me.*
ROBERT COOVER, *A Night at the Movies.*
STANLEY CRAWFORD, *Log of the S.S. The Mrs Unguentine.*
Some Instructions to My Wife.
RENÉ CREVEL, *Putting My Foot in It.*
RALPH CUSACK, *Cadenza.*
NICHOLAS DELBANCO, *Sherbrookes.*
The Count of Concord.
NIGEL DENNIS, *Cards of Identity.*
PETER DIMOCK, *A Short Rhetoric for Leaving the Family.*
ARIEL DORFMAN, *Konfidenz.*
COLEMAN DOWELL, *Island People.*
Too Much Flesh and Jabez.
ARKADII DRAGOMOSHCHENKO, *Dust.*
RIKKI DUCORNET, *Phosphor in Dreamland.*
The Complete Butcher's Tales.

RIKKI DUCORNET (cont.), *The Jade Cabinet.*
The Fountains of Neptune.

WILLIAM EASTLAKE, *The Bamboo Bed.*
Castle Keep.
Lyric of the Circle Heart.

JEAN ECHENOZ, *Chopin's Move.*

STANLEY ELKIN, *A Bad Man.*
Criers and Kibitzers, Kibitzers and Criers.
The Dick Gibson Show.
The Franchiser.
The Living End.
Mrs. Ted Bliss.

FRANÇOIS EMMANUEL, *Invitation to a Voyage.*

PAUL EMOND, *The Dance of a Sham.*

SALVADOR ESPRIU, *Ariadne in the Grotesque Labyrinth.*

LESLIE A. FIEDLER, *Love and Death in the American Novel.*

JUAN FILLOY, *Op Oloop.*

ANDY FITCH, *Pop Poetics.*

GUSTAVE FLAUBERT, *Bouvard and Pécuchet.*

KASS FLEISHER, *Talking out of School.*

JON FOSSE, *Aliss at the Fire.*
Melancholy.

FORD MADOX FORD, *The March of Literature.*

MAX FRISCH, *I'm Not Stiller.*
Man in the Holocene.

CARLOS FUENTES, *Christopher Unborn.*
Distant Relations.
Terra Nostra.
Where the Air Is Clear.

TAKEHIKO FUKUNAGA, *Flowers of Grass.*

WILLIAM GADDIS, JR., *The Recognitions.*

JANICE GALLOWAY, *Foreign Parts.*
The Trick Is to Keep Breathing.

WILLIAM H. GASS, *Life Sentences.*
The Tunnel.
The World Within the Word.
Willie Masters' Lonesome Wife.

GÉRARD GAVARRY, *Hoppla! 1 2 3.*

ETIENNE GILSON, *The Arts of the Beautiful.*
Forms and Substances in the Arts.

C. S. GISCOMBE, *Giscome Road.*
Here.

DOUGLAS GLOVER, *Bad News of the Heart.*

WITOLD GOMBROWICZ, *A Kind of Testament.*

PAULO EMÍLIO SALES GOMES, *P's Three Women.*

GEORGI GOSPODINOV, *Natural Novel.*

JUAN GOYTISOLO, *Count Julian.*
Juan the Landless.
Makbara.
Marks of Identity.

HENRY GREEN, *Blindness.*
Concluding.
Doting.
Nothing.

JACK GREEN, *Fire the Bastards!*

JIŘÍ GRUŠA, *The Questionnaire.*

MELA HARTWIG, *Am I a Redundant Human Being?*

JOHN HAWKES, *The Passion Artist.*
Whistlejacket.

ELIZABETH HEIGHWAY, ED., *Contemporary Georgian Fiction.*

AIDAN HIGGINS, *Balcony of Europe.*
Blind Man's Bluff.
Bornholm Night-Ferry.
Langrishe, Go Down.
Scenes from a Receding Past.

KEIZO HINO, *Isle of Dreams.*

KAZUSHI HOSAKA, *Plainsong.*

ALDOUS HUXLEY, *Antic Hay.*
Point Counter Point.
Those Barren Leaves.
Time Must Have a Stop.

NAOYUKI II, *The Shadow of a Blue Cat.*

DRAGO JANČAR, *The Tree with No Name.*

MIKHEIL JAVAKHISHVILI, *Kvachi.*

GERT JONKE, *The Distant Sound.*
Homage to Czerny.
The System of Vienna.

JACQUES JOUET, *Mountain R.*
Savage.
Upstaged.
MIEKO KANAI, *The Word Book.*
YORAM KANIUK, *Life on Sandpaper.*
ZURAB KARUMIDZE, *Dagny.*
JOHN KELLY, *From Out of the City.*
HUGH KENNER, *Flaubert, Joyce and Beckett: The Stoic Comedians.*
Joyce's Voices.
DANILO KIŠ, *The Attic.*
The Lute and the Scars.
Psalm 44.
A Tomb for Boris Davidovich.
ANITA KONKKA, *A Fool's Paradise.*
GEORGE KONRÁD, *The City Builder.*
TADEUSZ KONWICKI, *A Minor Apocalypse.*
The Polish Complex.
ANNA KORDZAIA-SAMADASHVILI, *Me, Margarita.*
MENIS KOUMANDAREAS, *Koula.*
ELAINE KRAF, *The Princess of 72nd Street.*
JIM KRUSOE, *Iceland.*
AYSE KULIN, *Farewell: A Mansion in Occupied Istanbul.*
EMILIO LASCANO TEGUI, *On Elegance While Sleeping.*
ERIC LAURRENT, *Do Not Touch.*
VIOLETTE LEDUC, *La Bâtarde.*
EDOUARD LEVÉ, *Autoportrait.*
Newspaper.
Suicide.
Works.
MARIO LEVI, *Istanbul Was a Fairy Tale.*
DEBORAH LEVY, *Billy and Girl.*
JOSÉ LEZAMA LIMA, *Paradiso.*
ROSA LIKSOM, *Dark Paradise.*
OSMAN LINS, *Avalovara.*
The Queen of the Prisons of Greece.
FLORIAN LIPUŠ, *The Errors of Young Tjaž.*
GORDON LISH, *Peru.*
ALF MACLOCHLAINN, *Out of Focus.*
Past Habitual.

The Corpus in the Library.
RON LOEWINSOHN, *Magnetic Field(s).*
YURI LOTMAN, *Non-Memoirs.*
D. KEITH MANO, *Take Five.*
MINA LOY, *Stories and Essays of Mina Loy.*
MICHELINE AHARONIAN MARCOM, *A Brief History of Yes.*
The Mirror in the Well.
BEN MARCUS, *The Age of Wire and String.*
WALLACE MARKFIELD, *Teitlebaum's Window.*
DAVID MARKSON, *Reader's Block.*
Wittgenstein's Mistress.
CAROLE MASO, *AVA.*
HISAKI MATSUURA, *Triangle.*
LADISLAV MATEJKA & KRYSTYNA POMORSKA, EDS., *Readings in Russian Poetics: Formalist & Structuralist Views.*
HARRY MATHEWS, *Cigarettes.*
The Conversions.
The Human Country.
The Journalist.
My Life in CIA.
Singular Pleasures.
The Sinking of the Odradek.
Stadium.
Tlooth.
HISAKI MATSUURA, *Triangle.*
DONAL MCLAUGHLIN, *beheading the virgin mary, and other stories.*
JOSEPH MCELROY, *Night Soul and Other Stories.*
ABDELWAHAB MEDDEB, *Talismano.*
GERHARD MEIER, *Isle of the Dead.*
HERMAN MELVILLE, *The Confidence-Man.*
AMANDA MICHALOPOULOU, *I'd Like.*
STEVEN MILLHAUSER, *The Barnum Museum.*
In the Penny Arcade.
RALPH J. MILLS, JR., *Essays on Poetry.*
MOMUS, *The Book of Jokes.*
CHRISTINE MONTALBETTI, *The Origin of Man.*
Western.

NICHOLAS MOSLEY, *Accident.*
Assassins.
Catastrophe Practice.
A Garden of Trees.
Hopeful Monsters.
Imago Bird.
Inventing God.
Look at the Dark.
Metamorphosis.
Natalie Natalia.
Serpent.

WARREN MOTTE, *Fables of the Novel:*
French Fiction since 1990.
Fiction Now: The French Novel in the
21st Century.
Mirror Gazing.
Oulipo: A Primer of Potential Literature.

GERALD MURNANE, *Barley Patch.*
Inland.

YVES NAVARRE, *Our Share of Time.*
Sweet Tooth.

DOROTHY NELSON, *In Night's City.*
Tar and Feathers.

ESHKOL NEVO, *Homesick.*

WILFRIDO D. NOLLEDO, *But for*
the Lovers.

BORIS A. NOVAK, *The Master of*
Insomnia.

FLANN O'BRIEN, *At Swim-Two-Birds.*
The Best of Myles.
The Dalkey Archive.
The Hard Life.
The Poor Mouth.
The Third Policeman.

CLAUDE OLLIER, *The Mise-en-Scène.*
Wert and the Life Without End.

PATRIK OUŘEDNÍK, *Europeana.*
The Opportune Moment, 1855.

BORIS PAHOR, *Necropolis.*

FERNANDO DEL PASO, *News from*
the Empire.
Palinuro of Mexico.

ROBERT PINGET, *The Inquisitory.*
Mahu or The Material.
Trio.

MANUEL PUIG, *Betrayed by Rita*
Hayworth.

The Buenos Aires Affair.
Heartbreak Tango.

RAYMOND QUENEAU, *The Last Days.*
Odile.
Pierrot Mon Ami.
Saint Glinglin.

ANN QUIN, *Berg.*
Passages.
Three.
Tripticks.

ISHMAEL REED, *The Free-Lance*
Pallbearers.
The Last Days of Louisiana Red.
Ishmael Reed: The Plays.
Juice!
The Terrible Threes.
The Terrible Twos.
Yellow Back Radio Broke-Down.

JASIA REICHARDT, *15 Journeys Warsaw*
to London.

JOÃO UBALDO RIBEIRO, *House of the*
Fortunate Buddhas.

JEAN RICARDOU, *Place Names.*

RAINER MARIA RILKE,
The Notebooks of Malte Laurids Brigge.

JULIÁN RÍOS, *The House of Ulysses.*
Larva: A Midsummer Night's Babel.
Poundemonium.

ALAIN ROBBE-GRILLET, *Project for a*
Revolution in New York.
A Sentimental Novel.

AUGUSTO ROA BASTOS, *I the Supreme.*

DANIËL ROBBERECHTS, *Arriving in*
Avignon.

JEAN ROLIN, *The Explosion of the*
Radiator Hose.

OLIVIER ROLIN, *Hotel Crystal.*

ALIX CLEO ROUBAUD, *Alix's Journal.*

JACQUES ROUBAUD, *The Form of*
a City Changes Faster, Alas, Than the
Human Heart.
The Great Fire of London.
Hortense in Exile.
Hortense Is Abducted.
Mathematics: The Plurality of Worlds of
Lewis.
Some Thing Black.

RAYMOND ROUSSEL, *Impressions of Africa.*

VEDRANA RUDAN, *Night.*

PABLO M. RUIZ, *Four Cold Chapters on the Possibility of Literature.*

GERMAN SADULAEV, *The Maya Pill.*

TOMAŽ ŠALAMUN, *Soy Realidad.*

LYDIE SALVAYRE, *The Company of Ghosts.*
The Lecture.
The Power of Flies.

LUIS RAFAEL SÁNCHEZ, *Macho Camacho's Beat.*

SEVERO SARDUY, *Cobra & Maitreya.*

NATHALIE SARRAUTE, *Do You Hear Them?*
Martereau.
The Planetarium.

STIG SÆTERBAKKEN, *Siamese.*
Self-Control.
Through the Night.

ARNO SCHMIDT, *Collected Novellas.*
Collected Stories.
Nobodaddy's Children.
Two Novels.

ASAF SCHURR, *Motti.*

GAIL SCOTT, *My Paris.*

DAMION SEARLS, *What We Were Doing and Where We Were Going.*

JUNE AKERS SEESE,
Is This What Other Women Feel Too?

BERNARD SHARE, *Inish.*
Transit.

VIKTOR SHKLOVSKY, *Bowstring.*
Literature and Cinematography.
Theory of Prose.
Third Factory.
Zoo, or Letters Not about Love.

PIERRE SINIAC, *The Collaborators.*

KJERSTI A. SKOMSVOLD,
The Faster I Walk, the Smaller I Am.

JOSEF ŠKVORECKÝ, *The Engineer of Human Souls.*

GILBERT SORRENTINO, *Aberration of Starlight.*
Blue Pastoral.
Crystal Vision.

Imaginative Qualities of Actual Things.
Mulligan Stew. Red the Fiend.
Steelwork.
Under the Shadow.

MARKO SOSIČ, *Ballerina, Ballerina.*

ANDRZEJ STASIUK, *Dukla.*
Fado.

GERTRUDE STEIN, *The Making of Americans.*
A Novel of Thank You.

LARS SVENDSEN, *A Philosophy of Evil.*

PIOTR SZEWC, *Annihilation.*

GONÇALO M. TAVARES, *A Man: Klaus Klump.*
Jerusalem.
Learning to Pray in the Age of Technique.

LUCIAN DAN TEODOROVICI,
Our Circus Presents...

NIKANOR TERATOLOGEN, *Assisted Living.*

STEFAN THEMERSON, *Hobson's Island.*
The Mystery of the Sardine.
Tom Harris.

TAEKO TOMIOKA, *Building Waves.*

JOHN TOOMEY, *Sleepwalker.*

DUMITRU TSEPENEAG, *Hotel Europa.*
The Necessary Marriage.
Pigeon Post.
Vain Art of the Fugue.

ESTHER TUSQUETS, *Stranded.*

DUBRAVKA UGRESIC, *Lend Me Your Character.*
Thank You for Not Reading.

TOR ULVEN, *Replacement.*

MATI UNT, *Brecht at Night.*
Diary of a Blood Donor.
Things in the Night.

ÁLVARO URIBE & OLIVIA SEARS, EDS.,
Best of Contemporary Mexican Fiction.

ELOY URROZ, *Friction.*
The Obstacles.

LUISA VALENZUELA, *Dark Desires and the Others.*
He Who Searches.

PAUL VERHAEGHEN, *Omega Minor.*

BORIS VIAN, *Heartsnatcher.*